BLUE
SKYE

BLUE SKYE

LAEL LITTKE

SCHOLASTIC HARDCOVER

Scholastic Inc.
New York

Library of Congress Cataloging-in-Publication Data

Littke, Lael.
    Blue Skye / Lael Littke.
        p. cm.
    Summary: Eleven-year-old Skye, who has spent most of her life on the
road with her mother, finally discovers what it is like to have a real home
and family when her mother marries and leaves Skye with her grandfather.

ISBN 0-590-43448-9

    [1. Mothers and daughters—Fiction.   2. Grandfathers—Fiction.]
I. Title.
PZ7.L719B1   1991
[Fic]— dc20   90-8597
                                                                          CIP
                                                                          AC

12 11 10 9 8 7 6 5 4 3 2 1   1 2 3 4 5 6/9
                Printed in the U.S.A.   37
            First Scholastic printing, October 1991

BLUE
SKYE

ONE

·

SKYE WISHED REANNA WOULDN'T HAVE SE-
crets. She wanted to tell her so, but how do you
say to your own mother that you don't like what
she does? Reanna wouldn't like it. She'd always
said that one thing she wouldn't take was sass.

So Skye just sat there in the old car, with her
tattered map of the western states tacked to the
dashboard with chewing gum, trying to plot out
where they were headed.

She'd asked about it that morning when they
started out with all their belongings stowed in the
back of the old station wagon. But Reanna had
just grinned and said, "Guess."

Skye couldn't guess. Taking all their stuff was
no clue. They did that a lot, every time Reanna
decided it was time to move on to a new job in
a new town. They didn't have much. Reanna
didn't believe in collecting any more than they

1

could carry in the car, along with the tent and camping equipment they used when they couldn't afford a room.

So all Skye said was, "Are we meeting Bill someplace?"

Bill was Reanna's man friend whom she'd met in Steamboat Springs where they'd stayed for almost a full six months. Bill had roared off the day before on his rusty old motorcycle, bound for who knew where.

Reanna smiled and said, "Wait and see."

Which was all Skye could do. She knew Reanna meant the secrets to be kind of a game. You'd think now that Skye was eleven Reanna would know she was a little old for that kind of thing. She should realize that Skye could handle knowing where they were going, even if it was just to another faded furnished room in another town with an interesting name. Reanna always picked towns that had unusual names.

They traveled west all day, through Maybell and Elk Springs and Dinosaur in Colorado, and on into Utah where they stopped in Vernal to have hamburgers. It wasn't until they passed through Salt Lake City and headed north on Interstate 15 that Skye began to suspect where they were going. When they left the interstate south of Brigham City, she knew for sure.

"We're going to Idaho, to Sheep Creek," she said. "We're going to Grandpa's farm."

"Bingo." Reanna looked away from the highway long enough to grin at her.

"Why?"

Reanna's eyebrows lifted. "What kind of a question is that? Don't you want to see your grandfather?"

Skye sighed. It wasn't that she didn't want to see Grandpa. He was nice enough. But she hardly knew him. Reanna had taken her to Sheep Creek only twice that she could remember. Once when she was seven and then again two years ago when the two of them had gone to Sheep Creek for Grandma Abby's funeral.

"He's not sick, is he?"

"He's fine." They were going through a canyon where the road was two-laned and narrow, so Reanna didn't look at her. "I would have told you if something was wrong, Skye."

She wondered about that. But to question it would be sass.

"So is this just a visit?"

Reanna grinned. "Sort of."

Reanna wasn't going to tell her anything. Skye leaned forward and traced the road to Sheep Creek with her finger. She was just going to have to wait and find out later why they were going there.

As they wound through the mountains, Skye found that she had a lot of memories stored in her head that she didn't even know were there. Like the way the tall sunflowers grew along the edges of the road. How each little valley had its own creek flowing down to join the bigger stream named Sheep Creek, from which the mountain village where Grandpa lived got its name. Roads ran alongside the creeks to the farms in each valley, and the trick was to figure out which one would take them to Grandpa's house. Reanna knew, of course, but Skye couldn't remember for sure.

But she did remember the pretty red brick church that sat like an ornament on a high rise of ground, surrounded by well-kept lawns and weeping birches. A dirt road behind it led farther up the hill to the cemetery where Grandma Abby was buried.

She remembered the old yellow schoolhouse on another rise, its vacant windows staring down through the narrow valley as if watching for schoolchildren who no longer came. Reanna said it hadn't been used for almost fifty years, since the new school was built; but it was still there, sturdy and indestructible.

Like Grandpa's house. He'd been born there, and his father before him. In fact, Skye had been born there, too, although she knew Reanna had gathered her up and hit the road as soon as she could. That was after Reanna's divorce. After the

father Skye had never known had gone off somewhere.

Grandpa was standing under the big cottonwood trees on the edge of his lawn when they
got to his place, with his old dog Tarzan beside
him. They stood just the way they had the day
Reanna and Skye had left after Grandma Abby's
funeral. Skye had an odd feeling that they'd been
standing there ever since, frozen in a block of
loneliness, waiting for her and Reanna to return.
Grandpa was tall and thin, like the white house
that loomed behind him. He waved as they drove
into the yard. Tarzan wagged his tail tentatively
as if he meant to check them out before he gave
them his full-treatment welcome, which included
barking and hand-licking.

"Hi, Dad," Reanna said as they got out of the
car.

She made no move to touch him, which didn't
surprise Skye. Reanna was not a huggy person.

"How do, Reanna," Grandpa said. "Hello,
Sis."

That's what he called Skye. Sis. Never Skye.
The other times they'd been there Skye had wondered if he disapproved of her name, but now
she just accepted being Sis.

He didn't comment on how much she'd grown
or ask what grade she was in, which seemed to

Skye the only things some adults could figure out to say to kids. He just stood there, drooping a little as if he were carrying a heavy load, looking at her through eyes as blue as the sky overhead.

Eyes like her own.

"Sure glad to see you, Sis," he said.

"I'm glad to see you, too, Grandpa." Then she surprised herself by walking over and putting her arms around his waist. He seemed so lonely and she knew they wouldn't be staying there long with him. Reanna never stayed in one place for long.

His hands, bony and hard, tightened a little awkwardly across her back.

Now Tarzan burst into joyous barking, whirling his tail, leaping around them, slathering doggy kisses wherever his tongue could reach.

"Skye," Reanna called. "Come help me unload."

Skye moved away from Grandpa now, wondering if she had embarrassed him by the hug. Wondering if she'd embarrassed herself.

"How much are we unloading?"

"Everything." Reanna's voice was muffled as she dug into the boxes of clothes and dishes in the car.

"Even the tent and stuff?"

"That can stay. Take everything else inside the house."

Grandpa cleared his throat. "Esta came over yesterday and made the beds up fresh."

Skye remembered that Esta was one of Grandpa's three sisters. Two of the sisters lived right there in Sheep Creek. Unlike Grandpa, who had only Reanna, each sister had several children, and those children each had passels of kids. Reanna called them "Cousins by the Dozens" and said Skye was related to all of them, too. She'd tried to explain the relationships, about first cousins and first cousins once removed and second cousins and all that. But to Skye it had been like one of those complicated math problems that she never could figure out.

She hadn't cared anyway, since she'd never expected to see them again.

Grandpa was still talking to Reanna. "Sweetie brought over a loaf of her bread yesterday. Asked when you'd be getting here. Wants to see you."

"Skye and I will go for a visit," Reanna said.

Grandpa nodded. "Skye'll want to meet Jermer."

That was news to Skye. "Who's Jermer?"

"Jermer Golightly," Grandpa said. "Boy who stays at Sweetie's house. He's seven."

Seven! Why would she want to meet a seven-year-old boy?

"Esta and Belva'll be coming by tonight," Grandpa said to Reanna. "Want to talk about the weddin'. They're in a fuss about not having time to plan things."

Reanna glanced quickly at Skye, then nabbed

onto Grandpa's arm and towed him off a little way.

But it was too late. Skye had heard.

"Wedding?" she said. "What wedding?"

Grandpa stared at her, then looked at Reanna. "Haven't you told Sis about it?"

Reanna came over now and draped an arm over Skye's shoulders. "Skye likes secrets. She had fun all the way, guessing why we were coming here." She smiled down at Skye. "Bill and I are getting married, Skye. What do you think about that?"

The idea that Reanna and Bill might get married had occurred to Skye while they were still back in Steamboat Springs. It was all right with her. She liked Bill. "It's okay," she said. "When?"

"Exactly one week from today. Next Monday afternoon at five p.m."

Skye let that sink in. "But why here? Couldn't you and Bill have got married in Steamboat Springs?"

Reanna laughed. "Because of the family, silly. You want to be with your family on a day like that."

Family had never seemed to be a part of Reanna's life before. Skye felt uneasy without knowing why.

"Haven't you told Sis the rest of it?" Grandpa asked.

Reanna laughed again and turned away to give

Grandpa a look Skye couldn't see. Then she turned back and said, "The rest of it is that you're to be my maid of honor, and we'll have the wedding right over there by the creek, under the willows."

Skye looked where Reanna pointed. It was a pretty place for a wedding. And the idea of being a maid of honor appealed to her.

But Grandpa had his jaw clamped shut so tight that a muscle jumped in his cheek, and that made her suspect she hadn't been told all of Reanna's secrets yet.

She didn't get any more hints of what more there might be during the week, but she didn't really worry about it. She was involved in the wedding plans, which were exciting, and in the visits to the aunts' houses, which weren't. If there were other secrets, nobody else knew them or else they had been warned not to tell Skye.

It seemed as if everything was going to go on smoothly, and then she and Reanna and Bill would be heading off — to where? Was that the last of Reanna's secrets?

She didn't find out what the rest of it was until the day of the wedding. Not until Bill brought the wedding surprise and Skye went to tell Jermer Golightly about it.

Two

NORMALLY, SKYE WOULDN'T HAVE BEEN caught dead going to see Jermer Golightly. What did a going-to-be-twelve-in-five-more-months person like her have in common with a kid like that?

But she had to tell *somebody* about the wedding surprise, and Jermer was the only warm, living body within walking distance who didn't already know. Unless, of course, you counted Sweetie Farnsworth who took care of Jermer. Sweetie wouldn't do. She was an adult and would probably say, the way Grandpa'd done, that the wedding surprise was pure foolishness.

Skye headed up the path to the barn, then picked her way across the rocky calf pasture where if you weren't careful you could step on a sunning snake. A skinny black and white cat watched her from the top rail of a wooden fence. Or maybe the cat was just hoping to catch herself a snake. She looked as if she hadn't eaten for a while.

Skye ran past the dark chokecherry trees where the mossy spring was, and was just stepping onto the sagging little footbridge that spanned the creek when she heard Jermer singing.

She paused, listening. You could test Jermer's moods by listening to his singing, the way Grandpa tested the wind by wetting a finger and holding it up.

Jermer's singing wasn't the absolute worst Skye had ever heard, but it was close. It cut through the August afternoon's orchestra of crickets and cackling chickens and murmuring creek like a seatbelt buzzer. " 'Though deep'ning tri-YALLS come YOO-ur way,' " he rasped mournfully, " 'Puh-RESS on, press on. . . .' "

Skye slumped. Jermer was holding another funeral. What was it with the kid? She and Reanna had visited there at Sweetie's house twice since they'd come to Sheep Creek, and Skye knew of three other funerals he'd held. One had been for a dead bird, but the others were for a wornout flashlight battery and a full-of-holes sock.

Jermer would be in one of his gloomy moods, but even so he was better than nobody. What good was a surprise if you couldn't tell *somebody* about it?

Skye finished crossing the little bridge, opened the wooden gate, and walked past Sweetie Farnsworth's old green car that sagged down into a patch of the mint plants that filled her yard. A person couldn't help but step on the plants, which smelled like a whole field of Doublemint gum.

Jermer was crouched in his cemetery, which was in one corner of Sweetie's vegetable garden. You'd think a person who loved funerals would be gray and decayed-looking, but Jermer wasn't like that. Jermer looked like a peach, his flesh firm and rounded and pinkish-gold. His blond hair was cropped short, so much like peach fuzz that it made a person want to rub it.

He crouched there in the dirt in his faded blue overalls, his old blue backpack beside him. Skye hadn't ever seen him without that backpack.

"Jermer," she called. "Jermer, guess what?"

Jermer didn't even look up from the tiny grave he was digging with a teaspoon. "What?" he droned, without interest.

Skye flopped down beside the grave, careful not to disturb the neat rows of little rock tombstones. "You'll never in all this world guess what Bill brought to Reanna for a wedding present."

Jermer's forehead wrinkled. "Who's Reanna?"

"My *mother*, Jermer. I told you that."

Jermer still didn't look up. "If I had a mother, I'd call her Mother."

Skye stifled a sigh. She'd explained all about

Reanna before, but Sweetie had told her about Jermer's mother being dead, so she tried not to be too exasperated. "Reanna likes me to call her by her name because she's my best friend besides being my mother. She's only eighteen years older than I am." Reanna always made sure people knew that. "Now, think about the surprise. Just guess what Bill brought for Reanna. They're getting married today, you know. Bill and Reanna." She thought she'd remind him in case he'd forgotten that, too.

"I know. Sweetie says I have to go." Jermer plunged the teaspoon into the grave and scooped out more dirt. "I can't guess," he said. "What's the surprise?"

Skye lay back on the ground, crushing mint plants. The scent rose up and wrapped around her like a blanket. She closed her eyes, picturing the surprise. "Motorcycles," she said softly. "Twin black-and-silver Harley-Davidson motorcycles. That's what Bill gave her. I mean, he gave her one and then there's one for him, too."

She could hear Jermer suck in his breath. It was the kind of reaction she'd hoped for.

"Black and silver?" he whispered. "With black leather seats and little trunks on the back to put their stuff in?"

Skye nodded without opening her eyes. "Bill's friend brought them inside a U-Haul trailer, and Bill didn't tell Reanna what was in there. He made her stand right behind the trailer, and he said some poetry about you-and-me-my-love-and-the-open-road. Then he flang open the door."

"Flang?" Jermer said.

"There they were, those twin black-and-silver Harleys, sitting side by side in the trailer."

Jermer let his breath out in a long sigh.

Skye opened her eyes and sat up, hugging her knees. "Jermer, can you imagine riding through the summer's day on one of those Harleys with the wind blowing your hair? It's no more old station wagon for Reanna and me. We're going to go in style from now on. Reanna and Bill and I."

Jermer wiped his hands on the front of his overalls. "Not you," he said. "They aren't going to take you."

The words fell on Skye's ears like the thudding of clods of dirt on a coffin. She'd looked at those black-and-silver Harleys and wondered where she was going to ride. But she hadn't, not even once, let herself think they wouldn't take her with them. This *couldn't* be another of Reanna's secrets.

"I'll ride behind Reanna," she said, louder than she needed to. "Haven't you ever seen two people on a motorcycle, Jermer Golightly? There's plenty of room for me." There was, wasn't there? She'd seen motorcycles with two people on them. Lots of times.

14

Jermer shook his head slowly. "Sweetie *told* me. She said how nice it's going to be for me to have somebody nearby to be friends with."

"She wouldn't say a thing like that." How could Sweetie think Jermer would be a suitable friend for Skye? A little kid like Jermer. He had to be making that up.

"Well, she did say it," Jermer insisted. "Your grandpa told her when he rode his horse over here that you'd be staying for quite a spell."

That's the way Grandpa would say it, all right.

Skye put her hands over her ears. She wasn't going to listen to any more nonsense. That's all it was. Nonsense.

"You're making that up, Jermer. Reanna and I have never been apart a single day, not since I was born. We've gone everywhere together. Reanna and I. She needs me."

Maybe Reanna was thinking about settling down there in Sheep Creek, now that she was getting married to Bill. Maybe they were all going to stay there.

But Skye knew Reanna was too restless for that. Reanna needed to be free to head for the next place that sounded interesting, looking for the exciting job that was worth giving up your freedom for.

Certainly Reanna would never, *not ever* go off without her. They'd always been together, traveling around in their old station wagon.

15

Skye scrambled to her feet. "Just come to the wedding and watch us ride off together on those black-and-silver Harleys, Jermer. You'll see. I'll be there behind Reanna. Come and see it with your own eyes."

Jermer pulled a small box from his pocket, the kind little round notebook reinforcements come in. He picked up a dead horsefly that Skye hadn't noticed before. Putting it inside the box, he closed the lid and placed the tiny coffin in the hole he'd dug. He began to sing again." 'Though deep'ning tri-YALLS come YOO-ur way. . . .' "

"What do you know anyway, Jermer Go-lightly?" Skye shouted. "Nothing, that's what you know. Nothing."

Her heart pounding, she ran back past the old car sitting in the mint patch, through the wooden gate, over the sagging footbridge, and into the rocky calf pasture. This time she didn't even watch out for snakes. Let them watch out for themselves.

People were already arriving for the wedding by the time Skye got back to Grandpa's house. Ladies in summery flowered dresses were getting out of dusty cars.

Some of them were the aunts — Aunt Belva and Aunt Esta and Aunt Vernell, Grandpa's three older sisters. Aunt Esta and Aunt Belva lived close by, and Aunt Vernell lived in Preston, the nearest town that had stores and a library and service stations.

Even more of the people were the Cousins by the Dozens.

The three aunts and some of the cousins who were Reanna's age carried platters of meat and bowls of potato salad, which they put on the long tables somebody had brought from the church and set up in the shade of the cottonwood trees.

There weren't many men. Grandpa had warned Reanna about that.

"Men around here would feel right foolish coming to a weddin' held in a danged cow pasture," he'd said.

Reanna had shrugged. "It's *my* wedding," she'd said. "I'll have it where I please, and if they don't want to come they can stay home. Besides," she'd added, "it's not going to be in a cow pasture. It'll be by the creek."

Grandpa grunted. "Same difference, far as I can see."

He'd been right about the men, though. A few came, including Aunt Belva's husband and the husbands of some of the older cousins. There was Bill's friend who'd brought the motorcycles in the U-Haul trailer, and there were a couple of men whom Skye didn't know. But most of the people were the flowery-dressed ladies. There were a lot of them, more than just the aunts and the cousins Reanna's age. Neighbors, probably, coming out of curiosity, Skye thought, to see what new craziness Reanna Rallison was up to, returning to Sheep Creek for her wedding, and on a Monday, too. Whoever heard of a wedding on a Monday?

How many times had Reanna told Skye stories of the way eyebrows used to shoot to the top of foreheads over the things she did? That was one reason she'd left Sheep Creek and the whole state of Idaho far behind in the first place, Reanna said.

It wasn't even sensible to think she'd abandon Skye there now.

Now wasn't the time to ask her. Reanna was running around Grandpa's broad lawn, directing the ladies where to put all the food they were bringing. She was already wearing what she was to be married in, a full-skirted white dress covered with bright-colored embroidery. She and Skye had each bought one like that when they were in Mexico two years ago, long before Reanna met Bill. Back then they'd liked to dress alike. Reanna said they looked like sisters.

But Skye had grown out of her dress. To be Reanna's bridesmaid today she'd be wearing something she'd found in the attic. It was a long summer-green dress that had been Reanna's prom dress when she was in high school. Grandma Abby — Reanna's mother — had packed it carefully away before she'd died. It was still pretty, and even though it was a trifle too big, Skye had chosen to wear it. The color looked good with her brown hair that was so much like Reanna's, except it had more red highlights to it. Reanna said she got that from her father whom Skye had never seen. She'd never even seen a picture of him. Reanna didn't believe in keeping old pictures. "Why drag your past along with you?" she said. "Leave it behind."

"Get dressed," Reanna mouthed to her now across the tables, which were loaded down with the meat and salads, as well as casseroles and cakes and Tupperware containers filled with Jell-O.

So Skye went inside the tall, narrow white house and climbed the stairs to the sunny, daisy-papered bedroom that had been Reanna's during her growing-up years. The green dress was there, and a garland made from the summer flowers Reanna had picked in the yard. They were both going to wear garlands in their hair, which Reanna had Frenchbraided when they first got up that morning.

As she dressed, Skye looked out of the upstairs window, just to keep an eye on Reanna and Bill. She couldn't see them, but she knew they were there, somewhere under the tall cottonwood trees. The battered station wagon was there, too. Reanna was going to leave it there, Skye guessed, when the three of them — Reanna and Bill and Skye — left on the shiny new motorcycles. Skye would miss that old car, which seemed more like home than any of the rented rooms she and Reanna had lived in. She even knew how to drive it, since Reanna'd taught her how in case of an emergency.

Beyond the tall trees the farmlands stretched across the valley and partway up the sagebrush-covered Idaho mountains.

From the window Skye could see Sweetie and Jermer crossing the rocky calf pasture, heading for the wedding. And there was Bill now, tall and broad-shouldered, pushing one of the wedding-present black-and-silver Harley-Davidsons across the lawn. He parked it near the food tables, then went and got the other one, which had his tent tied to it. The tent that was too small for three people. Skye scrubbed that thought out of her mind and watched Reanna come to stand beside Bill. They smiled at one another, each caressing the black leather seat of a Harley.

For the first time Skye felt excluded. Separate. Alone. They didn't need her.

Was it really possible that Reanna meant to leave her behind? She fastened the last button on the front of the green dress, put on her scuffed brown sandals, and quickly settled the garland on her head. It was time to go to the wedding.

THREE

SKYE HELD UP HER SKIRT AS SHE RAN DOWN-
stairs. The green dress was too long as well as
too big. If Reanna wanted her to change, she
would. She wouldn't be pigheaded about it. The
two of them had had a few little disagreements
lately, but Reanna said it was just adolescence
sneaking up on Skye.

But that wasn't enough to make Reanna want
to run off and leave her, was it?

Grandpa was on the wide front porch talking
to one of his sisters when Skye got downstairs.
Or rather, the sister was talking to him. Skye
wasn't sure which sister it was. She thought it
was the one named Esta, the oldest sister, whose
house she and Reanna had been at the day before
for a family dinner. But it could have been Vernell
or even Belva. Grandpa's three sisters all looked
alike, tall, with plump-pillow shapes and gray hair
permed and sprayed into rigid curls.

Whichever sister it was seemed upset.

"Well, of course you're going to do it," she said. "There can't be any question in your mind, Orville. It's your duty."

Now Skye knew which sister it was. Esta was the bossy one, and this one was bossy, all right.

Grandpa's shoulders sagged and his long face drooped. "Danged if I know what to do," he muttered. "Danged if I know."

The way he suddenly straightened when he saw her told Skye they'd been talking about her. So was she the duty Aunt Esta had been trumpeting about?

"Well, look who's here," Grandpa said. "Why, you sure look pretty, Sis."

Skye wanted to tell Grandpa that he could forget about duty since there was no way she was going to stay around here.

But she was superstitious about saying the words. Reanna always said that the things you put your tongue to were more likely to happen than those you just ignored.

Actually, she couldn't have gotten a word in even if she'd wanted to because Aunt Esta's jaw was still going.

"That dress is too big," Aunt Esta said. She marched over to Skye and began hitching it up at the neckline and yanking it in at the waist. "Don't you have something else you could wear, Skye? Something that fits you?"

"I like this dress," Skye said. Suddenly she liked it a *lot*. She liked it so much that she wasn't even going to ask Reanna about it being all right for the wedding. She was just going to wear it.

Aunt Esta went on. "Look at this, Orville. The girl is nothing but skin and bones. It's a disgrace, that's what it is. And there probably isn't any more to her mind than there is to her body, the way she never gets to stay in one school for more than a month or two."

Skye backed away, swelling with indignation. She was about to let Aunt Esta have it, demanding to know if any of *her* grandkids could identify the constellations in the sky, or the various types of geological formations, or give the botanical name for almost any plant in the forest, the way she could. Maybe she couldn't spell too well, and maybe she'd never win any prizes in math. But she'd learned all those other things from people she and Reanna'd met as they traveled around. She was going to holler that Aunt Esta's grandkids probably didn't know *anything* except maybe the names of their cows, but she didn't have the chance because just then Reanna came running lightly up the steps, her long braid swinging behind her.

"We'd better get things started," she said, glancing up at the dark clouds that were piling over the mountains. "It looks like rain's coming. Dad, would you get Tarzan tied up, please?"

23

Aunt Esta put her hands on her hips. "My stars, Orville, haven't you got that dog taken care of yet? It's a wonder he hasn't gobbled every morsel of food off the tables already."

"Ding, ding, ding," Grandpa muttered. But he hurried from the porch as if he were glad to have something to do.

"Skye," Reanna said. "Will you come with me? I've got something I need to talk with you about. Excuse us, Aunt Esta."

She held her hand out to Skye. After giving Aunt Esta a baleful glare, Skye took the hand, surprised at how cold it was. Reanna was nervous.

She took Skye around the house by the lilac bushes.

"You look nice," she said when they stopped.

"How nice?" Skye asked, playing their old game, wanting to put off what it was Reanna was going to say.

"As nice as gooseberries on pancakes with little plops of ice cream on top." Reanna reached out to twitch at the neckline of the summer-green dress. "Maybe we'd ought to take it in a little here."

"It's all right," Skye said. "I'll hold my shoulders back."

Reanna cleared her throat. "Skye, let me tell you about Bill's great idea. Remember how we told him about all the great places we've been to that have odd names? Like Wagontire, Oregon, and Cripple Creek, Colorado, and Twentynine Palms, California? Well, Bill wants to write a book about how they got their names and about interesting things that have happened in them. We're going to be traveling around to all kinds of places to do research."

Skye didn't say anything.

"We'll be going on our motorcycles," Reanna said. "We'll be riding south with the sun. South for the winter."

She paused.

"Is that what you wanted to talk to me about?" Skye asked.

Reanna twisted the pretty blue ring on her finger, the one Bill had given her when they decided to get married. "Well, kind of. See, we'll be on the move all the time."

"I'd like that," Skye said.

Reanna took a deep breath. "Skye, remember we've talked about how you'd ought to be getting a little continuity in your schooling? You can't get that, traveling around all the time the way we've been doing all your life. How would you feel about staying here with Grandpa? Just for a while. Not forever. That way you could be in one school for more than a couple of months."

She spoke fast, as if she wanted to get it all in before Skye could object.

"I'm not going to stay here," Skye said flatly.

25

It was just like Reanna to put off talking about this secret until the last minute.

"The aunts are worried about your education." Reanna went on as if she hadn't even heard Skye. "You'll be in the sixth grade this year and ought to be staying put in one place. You should make friends, too. Maybe even with all your cousins. Those Cousins by the Dozens." Reanna smiled at their old joke.

"Ick," Skye said.

"Skye, you've never had a chance to feel that you're part of a family, so don't judge it until you've tried it."

"The cousins don't like me. I'm not going to stay here."

"How do you mean the cousins don't like you?" Reanna ignored the important part of what Skye'd said.

"Remember yesterday at Aunt Esta's house? They didn't like me."

She knew why, too. She'd been bewildered and uneasy among all the relatives who'd gathered there at Aunt Esta's. Reanna had tried to point out who they all were — the gray-haired aunts and their bald husbands; their kids, who were Reanna's cousins and were all married; then there were *their* kids. That's the group where Skye was supposed to fit in. There were more of this younger group than Skye could hope to keep track of. They ranged from some who were teenagers to small babies who were passed around so much that it would take a genius to figure out whom they belonged to.

Two of the girls, Denise and Lee Esther, were going to be in the sixth grade like Skye, and Aunt Esta was determined that the three of them were going to be the best of friends.

"You're cousins," she'd said. "You all have the same blood. You'll get along just fine."

They were all related, all those people, all part of the same family.

"Think of them as a layer cake," Reanna'd said, "with your grandpa and the aunts in one layer, all of my cousins and me in the next, and all of *their* kids as the third layer, which includes you."

But Skye had still been confused and had sat there at Aunt Esta's as silent as a wart on a frog, not knowing what to say to anybody. Cody, a tall guy-cousin who Skye figured out was Denise's brother, had been friendly and had tried to make things easier for her. "Tell us about yourself, Skye," he'd said. "What do you like to do?"

Skye noticed some of the other cousins listening. What could she say that they might want to hear?

"I like to go places and see things," she said.

Cody nodded as if that was a fine thing to like to do. "Tell us about some of them."

Skye liked to talk about the places she and Reanna had been. They'd been to so many, staying until Reanna got the urge to be free again. Reanna said the most important thing in the world was to be free.

"Did you know there's a place called Ten Sleep in Wyoming?" Skye said. "And a town named Truth or Consequences in New Mexico?"

"You're kidding!" Cody said.

"No, really." Skye felt encouraged. "And I've been to Tombstone, Arizona, and Zigzag, Oregon. Then there's Dingle, Idaho, and Browse, Utah, and Hungry Horse, Montana."

"Have you been to Disneyland, California?" asked Lee Esther.

"Oh, yes," Skye began, but then she saw that Lee Esther was smirking. Denise grinned slyly and started whispering in Lee Esther's ear. They both giggled as they looked at Skye.

That was when Skye had realized they thought she was bragging, and they didn't like her for it.

But how could she explain all that to Reanna now when the wedding was about to start?

She didn't have to because just then Bill came around the corner of the house.

"There you are, Reanna," he said. "I didn't know what happened to you. Hi, Blue Skye."

That was his name for her, because of her blue eyes. He'd sung it to her the first time Reanna had introduced them, back in Steamboat Springs. " 'Blue Skye, smiling at me,' " he'd sung while strumming on an imaginary guitar. He'd said it was from an old song.

"Hi," Skye said, relieved that he'd interrupted the miserable conversation.

Bill was dressed in a white shirt over dark pants. The shirt had lots of white embroidery on the front, and four pockets. Reanna had sent off to Mexico to get it for the wedding.

One of the aunts had made a big fuss about him having his shirt hanging out, but Reanna told her that was the way it was supposed to be worn. "It's a Mexican wedding shirt," she'd said.

Skye thought he looked nice.

"The flutes are here," Bill said.

Reanna nodded. "Then let's get started before it rains. Skye, think about what I said. You'll like it here."

"*You* didn't," Skye said. "You said it was like a prison here on Grandpa's farm, a million miles from anywhere. You said you didn't like the aunts butting into your business all the time. You *said*."

Reanna sighed. "Will you go now and tell Grandpa and the aunts to get ready for the procession?"

"Okay. But I'm not staying." Skye gathered up her skirt and started off, but stopped again when she heard Bill whisper, "I guess you told her."

Suddenly things came clear. It was Bill who

was behind this scheme to leave her. She should have known when he came with those two Harleys. He was thinking *two* people, not three. He didn't want her along with them. He wanted Reanna to himself.

Well, let them *try* to get away without her. Just let them try.

FOUR

IF IT HADN'T BEEN FOR HER KNOWLEDGE THAT Reanna and Bill were really going to try to leave her, Skye would have enjoyed the wedding. It began with a procession, led by two girls playing flutes. They wore flower garlands on their heads like Reanna's and Skye's. Next came Reanna and Bill, followed by Bill's friend who'd brought the motorcycles, then Skye and Grandpa who smelled of shaving lotion and Listerine. He walked stiffly, as if he disapproved of the whole thing, which Skye knew he did.

Then there were all the aunts, uncles, and those Cousins by the Dozens. Denise was there in a cream-colored dress that made her black hair look even darker, and Lee Esther was there, too, in a blue dress that didn't do a whole lot for her pale brown hair and sunburned skin. Both of them had their hair sprayed so much that it stood out around their faces like wire. Both of them wore

31

nylons and white shoes with little heels.

Looking at them Skye felt like a geek in the droopy long green dress and her floppy old sandals. But Cody, the tall guy-cousin who'd been nice to her at Aunt Esta's, grinned and winked at her, which made her feel a little better. There was another guy with Cody, younger, about Skye's age, with red hair and freckles. He glanced at Skye and blushed.

She guessed that he must be one of the neighbors' kids.

The other wedding guests trailed behind the relatives. Jermer Golightly and Sweetie Farnsworth were back there somewhere. Jermer wore a tight-fitting dark blue suit with too-short sleeves. For once he didn't have his backpack with him. Sweetie was dressed in something magenta-colored and flowing, a lot different from the pale, flowered dresses the aunts wore. Her hair, which was a mixture of blonde and gray, was done up in a smooth lump at the back of her head. She seemed a lot younger than the aunts.

They all walked across Grandpa's wide lawn and down the long shady lane that led to the creek. The flutes played something light and happy that made you want to dance. Except that Skye felt too heavy to dance. Heavy with the knowledge that Bill didn't want her along. It began to hurt now, like when you pound a finger but there's no pain right at first. Then, just when you think, "Well, that wasn't so bad," it pounces on you and makes you scream.

Bill didn't want her, and Reanna was willing to toss her away like those pictures from the past that she'd got rid of.

Well, Skye didn't care. She'd show them all. They weren't going to get away with this. She had a secret of her own.

She clumped along, hitching up the neck of her dress and thinking angrily about how she was going to let off quite a mouthful when they got to that part of the marriage ceremony about speak now or forever hold your peace. She'd seen weddings on the TV soap operas she and Reanna watched. She'd wait until they asked if anybody knew a reason why this marriage shouldn't happen. Then she'd really let them have it.

She scarcely noticed when Sweetie Farnsworth caught up with her.

"That scooped neck is going to scoop right down to your belly button if you're not careful," Sweetie whispered. Skillfully she pulled the front of the dress together and fastened it with an old-fashioned brooch she'd been wearing on her own dress. "Now you look like a bridesmaid," she whispered as she dropped back to join Jermer.

The ceremony was short. It took place under a bower of willows by the creek. Several cows and a couple of horses watched from behind a fence across the creek. That skinny black and white cat was there, too, roosting on the trunk of a fallen tree where it had a good view of everything.

Back at the house Tarzan barked, unhappy about being left behind.

Reanna and Bill stood together under the willows, with Bill's friend on one side and Skye on the other. They said some poetry to one another and exchanged wedding rings while Skye held Reanna's bouquet. Then they signed some papers that an official-looking man had brought. That's all there was to it. They were married. Nobody even said anything about speaking now or forever holding your peace.

Bewildered, Skye walked behind the newlyweds back to the lawn where the aunts and uncles and Cousins by the Dozens and other guests swarmed over the food tables, squawking like the magpies that picked through Grandpa's manure pile by the barn.

The cousin named Cody had some pieces of cardboard and a big felt pen.

"Let's make some 'Just Married' signs, Skye," he said, giving her the pen. "We can tie them to the motorcycles."

Skye had no interest in making signs, but she took the piece of cardboard Cody held out to her and started printing.

Denise and Lee Esther and several younger cousins watched.

It made Skye nervous. Her hand shook.

She'd just finished printing one sign when Denise poked Lee Esther and said in a loud whisper, "Maybe they don't teach spelling in Ten Sleep and Tombstone and those other fancy places she's been."

Lee Esther tossed her pale, stiff hair and smiled. "Denise's the spelling champion of the whole county," she said, as if that meant something great.

Skye looked at the sign and saw she'd printed, "Just Marred." How could she have done anything that dumb right in front of the cousins?

"You can fix that easy," Cody said.

But Skye handed him the pen. "You fix it." She couldn't keep her mind on dumb signs. Reanna and Bill would be leaving soon.

She hurried upstairs where she took off the green dress and the garland and put on her jeans and old red plaid shirt. That was what she always wore for traveling. She put the garland of flowers back on her head. That would remind Reanna of all the years they'd traveled together, stopping to pick roadside flowers and braid them together.

Shoving her few possessions into her duffel, Skye started downstairs. She wasn't even halfway down when she heard the engines of the black-and-silver Harleys rev up.

"Skye," she heard Reanna call. "Skye, come say good-bye."

Skye clattered down the rest of the stairs. "I'm coming, Reanna," she yelled. "Wait for me."

The cycles were already moving by the time she got out to the yard.

"Wait," she screamed. "I'm going with you."

"Come give me a hug," Reanna said, reaching out her arms. Skye plunged into them. "Hey, pal," Reanna whispered in her ear, "I sure love ya."

"How much?" This was another of their old games. It was a baby game, but Skye wanted to jog Reanna's memory about all those things they'd shared.

Reanna laughed softly.

"As much as from here to Tincup, Colorado. This is hard, honeybun. We've never been apart before." Reanna tried to pry Skye off of her. Reanna never was much of a toucher.

But Skye clung to her, still clutching her duffel. "Take me with you. I can't stay here."

"Yes, you can. Now smile, Skye, and tell me you're happy for me." Reanna unwound her arms. For just a moment she looked into her eyes and Skye thought she was going to relent and say, "Aw, what the heck. Hop on behind me."

But all she said was, "Good-bye, Skye. Good-bye, my dearie, my daughter."

Now Skye was supposed to say, "Good-bye, my mother, my dear."

But she wasn't going to say that now. That was

for when Reanna went to work and would be home at the end of the day.

"Good-bye, Skye," Bill echoed.

The motorcycles started rolling again.

Dumping the duffel, Skye ran after them wailing, "I'm not staying. I'm not staying." She even got a leg up on Reanna's cycle, but Bill reached over and gently lifted her off.

"Sorry, Blue Skye," he said with that big goofy grin she used to like. "No kids allowed on the honeymoon." Reaching behind him, he pulled a new map of the western states from a pocket on his cycle. "Here, you can follow us on this map. We'll let you know where we're heading."

He thrust it into Skye's hand and hugged her.

She yanked away. She didn't want his hugs and she didn't want his stupid map. She picked it up and threw it back at him. "I've already got a map," she yelled.

"Skye, listen," Reanna said without stopping her motorcycle. "Get acquainted with the cousins and everybody, and you'll hardly notice we're gone. We'll be back soon."

"How soon?" Skye demanded. "Soon" was an elastic word with Reanna that could stretch to mean any amount of time she wanted it to mean. "Three days? Four?"

"Soon," Reanna repeated. "We'll be in touch. Be happy, Skye."

Then they were gone in a thunder of *vrooms* and clouds of dust.

"Four days," Skye screamed. "Be back in four days!" She tore the flower garland from her head and hurled it after them, sobbing with despair.

She was still sobbing when the sound of the cycles died away. The rest of the world was silent. Even Tarzan had stopped barking. Tied to his chain, he watched her.

So did everybody else. One of those Cousins by the Dozens snickered.

Skye didn't turn around.

Jermer came out of the crowd to take her hand. He led her to where the wilting garland lay, powdered now with dust.

He picked it up. "Let's go bury it," he said.

Without even looking at those Cousins by the Dozens, she followed him up through the calf pasture, past the chokecherry grove where the spring was, and through the wooden gate to his cemetery.

Jermer got a shovel and dug a grave. Skye dropped in the wilted garland. They both pushed the dirt in to cover it up.

Sweetie Farnsworth came puffing along just in time to put her arms around them and join in singing, " 'Though deep'ning tri-YALLS come your way. . . .' "

The scent of mint rose up around them strong enough to make a person's eyes water.

FIVE

SKYE PLANNED TO CRY ALL NIGHT LONG.

She tried hard as she lay in her bed in the narrow, slant-ceilinged upstairs room, but after a few dry sobs she gave it up. She wasn't a crier. Just because she'd cried when Reanna and Bill rode away didn't mean she was a wimpy weeper. She'd had a good reason to cry. Even old spelling champ Denise would have cried if *her* mother had left her behind.

She stared into the darkness, hanging onto the thought that Reanna and Bill would be back in three or four days. But *she* was the one who said they'd be back then. Not Reanna. She didn't think Reanna would have made it such a big secret if they were going to be gone only three or four days.

What if they were gone a month?

Skye groaned.

What she really should do was figure out how

to catch up to them. They wouldn't be going far that night, especially since it was starting to rain.

She and Reanna had passed a pretty place to camp alongside Bear River on the day they'd arrived in Sheep Creek. It was just a few miles away on the road to Preston. That's probably where Reanna and Bill would be camping, at least that night.

If she could find them and showed up right at their tent, they wouldn't turn her away. Or would they?

An imagined scene of them pushing her out of their tent into the darkness almost brought the tears. She thought of the "Fanged Haunts" Reanna used to tell her about when she was small. They were creatures that inhabited the darkness beyond the campfire, ready to gobble up foolish children who wandered away from safety. She wasn't quite sure what Fanged Haunts were supposed to look like, but Reanna had said they were out there, with gaping, fanged mouths ready.

She imagined Reanna and Bill throwing her out of the tent, with the Fanged Haunts there, waiting, their eyes glowing like stars and their breath whispering in and out like the night wind in the trees.

One big sob was all she could manage. She tried to stay awake and figure out how she could go after Reanna. Forget Bill. She'd just ignore him.

But the bed was firm and comfortable, not at all like the squashy, lumpy cots in the rented rooms where she and Reanna had lived. The sheets were crisp and smelled of sunshine and fresh air, not stale like the old sleeping bags they'd used when they camped.

She slept.

She woke in the morning to the sound of raindrops on the roof. She lay there looking at the daisies on the pale green wallpaper and thinking of Reanna and Bill camped somewhere in the rain, soggy and miserable. But then she remembered the cozy days she and Reanna had spent in their tent, playing games, talking, making plans while the rain pattered against the canvas.

Suddenly she felt as dismal as the day.

Then she heard the sound that told her how she could escape to go looking for Reanna and Bill. Grandpa was bringing the full milk cans to the roadside where Mr. Jensen, the milk hauler, would pick them up. Sometimes people used Mr. Jensen's truck like a bus service, riding into Preston with him to do some shopping, then riding home with him on his return trip.

Skye had met Mr. Jensen twice in the week she'd been in Sheep Creek. He would let her ride along with him, and she'd see those black-and-silver Harleys somewhere along the way.

She'd better not tell Grandpa. He'd probably be happy to have her leave, but he'd feel it was his duty to stop her. She and Reanna could call him later from town.

Now that she had a plan, Skye jumped out of bed, and looked right into the face of a Fanged Haunt that perched on the windowsill, on the other side of the glass. That's what it had to be, sitting there dripping and ugly in the rain with its open mouth displaying small but nasty fangs.

"Reanna, help!" Skye whispered through a dry throat.

The Fanged Haunt disappeared, but not before Skye saw it was just the skinny black and white cat again, the one that had been watching her since she came.

She ran to the window, feeling embarrassed, as if somebody had caught her believing in the tooth fairy. The cat stood on a limb of the huge tree just outside the window, and again it opened its mouth in a silent meow.

"Here, kitty, kitty." Skye pushed up the window, but the cat skittered down the trunk of the tree and vanished in the rain.

Mr. Jensen's milk truck went by on its way to the farms on the north end of the village, which meant Skye had about an hour to get ready to leave. That was plenty of time.

She got dressed, once again putting on her traveling outfit of jeans, red plaid shirt, and sneakers. Her duffel was still packed from yesterday. On her way downstairs, she stashed it along with her map of the western states and her denim jacket on the landing.

Grandpa was just sitting down at the kitchen table with his newspaper. "Well, good morning, Sis," he said when he saw her.

This was the first time the two of them had had breakfast alone. He looked as if he was trying to think of something else to say. Finally he said, "Better have some breakfast," and unfolded the newspaper, which he put up in front of his face.

"I will." She didn't mind that he hid behind the newspaper. That way he wouldn't notice if she looked flushed or excited. She hoped he'd go back to the barn before Mr. Jensen returned. "Aren't you going to eat, Grandpa?" she asked.

"Yes, I am, Sis." Grandpa's arm snaked out from behind the newspaper. He picked up a bowl from the stack that always sat on the table, then fumbled for one of the cereal boxes that were also stored there.

Breakfast with Grandpa was simply taking your pick of the many boxes of cereal that occupied half of the light-colored oval table. Twice since Skye and Reanna had been there Aunt Esta had come over and put all of the cereal boxes inside one of the cupboards. Both times, as soon as she'd gone, Grandpa took them all out again and put them back on the table.

Skye took a bowl from the stack and looked over the selection of cereals. There were Shredded Wheat and Corn Flakes and All-Bran and some others equally dull. Grandpa didn't go for the interesting ones like Cocoa Puffs and Cinnamon Toast Crunch, although Skye'd found a box of Crispy Critters.

After a look out the window to make sure Mr. Jensen wasn't coming back yet, she filled her bowl half full of Crispy Critters and added milk from the thick white pitcher that stood on the table. Milk from Grandpa's own cows. She poured some on Grandpa's All-Bran, too.

While she ate, Skye kept an eye on the old-fashioned clock that sat on a shelf on the kitchen wall. The cabinet of the clock, which was almost two feet high, was wood, carved in sworls and leaves. There was a little glass door through which you could see a golden pendulum swinging back and forth, back and forth, measuring out the minutes and days and years. On each hour the clock bonged out the time of day.

Skye liked the clock. In fact, she liked the whole kitchen. She and Reanna had never had a real kitchen, although some of the rented rooms they'd lived in had a refrigerator and stove and sink. This kitchen was big, with room for a table and four chairs as well as a daybed along one wall. An old treadle sewing machine sat under the big double windows that looked out toward the highway. Skye remembered that when Grandma Abby was alive, there'd been bright-colored geraniums in pots on the windowsills. Grandpa said he had too many things to take care of, so he'd given them away.

"Jittery, Sis?" Grandpa asked suddenly, and Skye was aware that she'd been drumming her fingers while she ate her cereal.

She'd better act casual while she listened for Mr. Jensen's truck.

Clearing her throat, she said, "Grandpa, do you know where that cat lives? That scrawny one that hangs around and watches us?"

Grandpa was hiding behind his newspaper again. "Probably nowhere," he said around it.

"But it must live somewhere. Where did it come from if nobody owns it?"

"Sometimes people drop their unwanted animals off along the road. Danged fools think somebody will take them in, but there are too many of them." Grandpa lowered the newspaper a little. "Cat's just a stray. Lucky one at that, if Tarzan hasn't torn it apart."

Skye was horrified. "Would he do that?"

"Dunno. Doesn't generally take to having strays on his turf." Grandpa went back to reading his paper.

Did Grandpa resent having strays on *his* turf, too?

Well, she wouldn't be there much longer. Skye shoved the rest of her cereal into her mouth. It was stale, like the others in the boxes on the table.

How long had they been sitting there? How long did it take for one person to eat through nine boxes of cereal all by himself?

Maybe she'd ought to offer to fix breakfast for Grandpa. She and Reanna had invented some great things, like Cheese Monster, which was a Bisquick biscuit topped with Velveeta cheese and a fried egg. She knew how to make that.

But it wouldn't be fair to get Grandpa used to good cooking when she was cutting out. Besides, there wasn't time now.

Grandpa put down his newspaper and pushed his chair back, the legs scraping against the linoleum floor. "Got work to do out in the barn." Standing, he looked at Skye as if he were trying again to think of more to say. "See you later, Sis," he said, and left.

"Good-bye, Grandpa." Skye hoped he'd stay inside the barn so he wouldn't see her getting into the milk truck. She'd leave him a note. He'd understand how it was.

As she swallowed her last Crispy Critter, Skye saw the black and white cat loft itself to the windowsill outside. She was glad to know Tarzan hadn't gotten it.

The cat carried something in her mouth, something small and wet and bedraggled. A kitten! The skinny cat had a kitten.

"Oh, babe!" Skye murmured, leaping to her feet and hurrying outside. What if Tarzan should come before she got to the cat? Could he put his big paws up on the sill and snatch both the mother and the kitten?

Tarzan was nowhere in sight, but that didn't mean he couldn't show up at any moment.

The cat allowed Skye to pick her up and carry her inside, still holding the dripping kitten by the scruff of its neck. Skye put the cat down on the kitchen floor. Only then did the cat let go of the kitten, setting it down gently on its sturdy little legs.

The kitten was small. Skye didn't know a whole lot about cats, but she thought it was probably close to a month old. The marks on its face gave it a funny, surprised look. The black and white on its back made it look as if it were wearing overalls.

It stood there bewildered, turning its head and mewing in high-pitched squeaks.

Skye thought it was the most beautiful thing she'd ever seen. She'd never had a pet. "Pets are a nuisance," Reanna had said. "They tie you down."

There'd been that time they'd rented a room in a big two-story house in Wyoming, a house that had been full of kids and animals. The family cat had kittens, three bright orange and white ones, and one little tiger-striped gray one with green eyes. Skye had loved that little gray cat and had begged Reanna to let her take him when they left. Reanna explained patiently that the way they lived, traveling from place to place in the old station wagon, was no life for a kitten, that it needed cat food they couldn't afford, that taking on a responsibility like that was limiting their freedom.

Skye had said a tearful good-bye to the gray kitten when Reanna got bored with the waitress job she'd taken at a cafe in town and said it was time to move on. The kids at the house said they didn't know anybody who wanted a kitten. Their faces had been gloomy when they said it, as if they knew what happened to unwanted kittens. Skye hadn't wanted to know.

The skinny cat was licking her baby, glancing up now and then at Skye. She made soft, proud sounds, which Skye interpreted as meaning, "Isn't it splendid? Isn't it the most beautiful kitten you ever saw?"

Skye plopped down on the floor and reached out to pet the mother cat's wet fur. She was shocked at how thin the cat was. "Hey babe," she said. "You're just skin and bones." That was what Aunt Esta had said about her. "I'll get you something to eat."

But the cat wanted out. Walking over to the door, she meowed politely.

Skye got up. "You're going to run off without your baby? You're like somebody else I could name."

The cat threaded herself through Skye's feet, rubbing washboard ribs against her legs.

"Okay, if that's what you want." Skye opened the door and the cat dashed off in the rain.

It was then that she heard Mr. Jensen's truck coming back down the road.

"Hey, come back," she yelled at the cat. "I can't baby-sit for you. I have to go."

But the cat was gone.

Skye turned to look at the kitten who took trembling steps toward nowhere. It mewed frantically. Skye picked it up, making soft, soothing sounds.

The kitten was a male. The kids in that two-story house in Wyoming had taught her how to tell. He fit perfectly into her palm. She stroked his back with a gentle finger.

"I'll just have to put you back outside, I guess," she said.

But Tarzan might get him.

The kitten smelled clean, like the hay in Grandpa's barn. That must have been where the mother cat had been keeping him. Maybe she should take him back there.

But the barn wasn't safe with Tarzan there, which was probably why the mother cat had brought him to the house.

The milk truck was at the neighbor's place now. Skye could hear the whine of the lift that hoisted the heavy cans to the bed of the truck.

If she didn't go with Mr. Jensen this morning, Reanna and Bill would probably move on. To where? Which direction would they be going? How could she find them?

She peered through the rain, looking for the mother cat. "Kitty, kitty," she called.

The cat was nowhere in sight. Skye would just have to leave the kitten there in the kitchen and hope for the best.

Putting him back on the floor, she hurried to the stair landing for her things. She pulled on her denim jacket, grabbed her map, and threw the duffel over her shoulder. As she went out, she left the door open so the mother cat could get back in to her kitten.

Mr. Jensen's truck stopped at the end of the driveway to pick up Grandpa's milk cans.

Behind Skye the kitten mewed. She looked back. He stood alone on the doorsill, turning his head, blurry blue eyes searching. Was he trying to follow her?

She couldn't just leave him there. But he was too small to take with her.

Well, so the world was a hard place.

Mr. Jensen slammed a door as he got out of the truck. The noise must have frightened the kitten because he skittered back into the kitchen, still mewing.

Skye began to run toward the milk truck. "Mr. Jensen," she called.

Tarzan came from the barn to deliver a friendly bark at Mr. Jensen then looked curiously toward the house. Could he hear the kitten's tiny cries?

Skye stopped. She'd have to shut the kitchen door so Tarzan couldn't get in.

But then the mother cat couldn't get in either. Would Tarzan grab the cat while she tried to get to her baby?

Mr. Jensen looked toward Skye. "Did you want something, Skye?"

Maybe Reanna and Bill would stay put for a day or two since it was raining so hard. Maybe she could catch up with them tomorrow.

"Just wanted to say hello," Skye yelled to Mr. Jensen, then turned back toward the house.

SIX

BEHIND HER, SKYE HEARD MR. JENSEN'S
truck start up. She thought of it going down the
road, past the dripping willows that lined the
creek bank, past the church and the school and
the general store, past the gray cliffs that jutted
out toward the river. That's where she was sure
Bill and Reanna would be camped, there under
the giant box elder trees by the riverside, where
they could hear the whisper of the water as they
ate breakfast in their tent. Maybe they had
cooked bacon in the shelter of the big trees over
Reanna's little one-burner propane stove. The
smell of it would be strong in the tent, along with
the odors of the canvas and the freshness of the
rain-filled air.

So what was Skye doing here, worrying about
a dumb kitten? Why hadn't she believed Reanna,
who'd said so many times that pets tie you down,
limit your freedom, get in your way?

Skye was almost back to the kitchen door when Jermer Golightly suddenly appeared. He slogged through the rain juggling a huge black umbrella, his blue backpack, and an armful of boxes.

Great. That's just what she needed. Somebody who sang mournful songs and liked funerals.

Maybe he'd like to hold a funeral for her hopes.

Tarzan came over to wag his tail as a greeting to Jermer, then went back to the barn.

"Hi," Jermer said to Skye. "Want to play Boggle? I don't know how to spell many words, but I like to play."

Now Skye saw that the boxes Jermer carried were games. Monopoly. Clue. Scrabble. Some others whose titles she couldn't see.

"No," she said.

"How about Rook? Or Go Fish? I've got Pit, too, and Uno." Jermer followed her inside the kitchen, taking a while to get the big umbrella through the door, then kicking the door shut behind him. He stopped short when he heard the kitten mewing. Spotting him there in the middle of the floor, Jermer dropped the umbrella and tossed his backpack and armload of games on the table, falling to his knees beside the kitten. "Skye, where did you get him?"

"His mother dumped him on me," Skye said.

Jermer reached out a hand to stroke the mewing kitten. "He's so scared. Is it all right if I pick him up?"

Skye shrugged. "I couldn't care less."

Why was she angry at the kitten? He couldn't help being dumped any more than she could.

"He'd probably like it," she said in a kinder voice.

Jermer picked the kitten up, cradling him against his chest. "Oh, oh, oh," he crooned. "Oh, oh, oh." He looked at Skye. "What's his name?"

"You just named him," Skye said. "We'll call him Oh."

"Oh," Jermer sang. "Oh, Oh, Oh." It was the tune from the funeral song Jermer liked to sing.

"Want him?" Skye asked.

For a moment Jermer's face lit up, but then he said, "I couldn't take him to Sweetie's house. Old Mangler would chew him up."

Mangler was Sweetie Farnsworth's old tomcat. Skye had seen him, a battered orange warrior with half a tail and one droopy ear. Sweetie said she'd found him somewhere, hurt, near death, and had brought him home to see what she could do. Now he was fat and lazy and jealous of his territory.

Like Tarzan.

What difference did it make whether Mangler chewed up the kitten or if Tarzan got to him first?

"Besides," Jermer said, "he's too young to be away from his mother."

"His mother's gone," Skye said.

Jermer held the kitten against his cheek and

smiled, a soft, sweet smile. "She'll come back," he said. "Cats always do."

As if in answer to his certainty, there was a meow at the door. Skye hurried over to open it. The scrawny cat picked up a kitten she'd apparently dropped so she could meow, and brought it inside. Setting it down at Skye's feet, she looked up.

"Sure," Skye said. "Why not? You've already ruined my life. I might as well take in another kitten."

Despite her harsh words, she knelt to look at the new arrival. This one was smaller than Oh, but it stood its ground silently, and when Skye touched it gently, it opened its tiny mouth and hissed.

Skye fell instantly, hopelessly in love. "Oh, you little thing," she said. "You sassy little thing."

She picked up the kitten. Like the other one, this one was mostly black, but it had a white face and chest and a little black chin which gave it a flower look. It stood on Skye's palm and stared at her through blue eyes blurred with babyhood. It hissed again.

"No bigger than a Twinkie, but ready to fight," Skye said.

That's what she'd name this one. Twinkie. When Reanna saw the spirit of the little thing, she'd let her keep it. Reanna admired spirit, especially in females. Skye checked and wasn't surprised to find that's what this kitten was. Surely Reanna would say they had to keep this one.

Happier than she'd been for a good twenty-four hours, Skye looked around for the mother cat. Maybe she'd eat now that she'd brought her kittens inside.

But the cat was gone.

"She went outside again," Jermer said. "Probably after more kittens."

Skye felt weak. What was she going to do with the other kittens? There was a possibility Reanna would let her keep Twinkie, but she might as well forget right now about asking for more.

Jermer couldn't take them. He'd already said old Mangler would never allow that.

Grandpa maybe? Would he keep a watch on the kittens so Tarzan wouldn't get them? But he already had too much to take care of.

The aunts? No, Skye had been in Aunt Esta's house and knew she was a ferocious housekeeper who'd never allow animals and probably only a few humans to walk on her shiny clean floors. Very likely the other aunts were the same way.

She wondered if Cody liked kittens. Maybe she could make friends with Denise and Lee Esther, and they'd each take a kitten.

Jermer interrupted her thoughts. "We'd better fix them a house. If we let the kittens run around on the floor, somebody's going to squish them."

He rocked little Oh soothingly as he crooned that dreary funeral song.

Holding Twinkie against her chest, Skye went to the back porch and found a pasteboard box. A little rooting around uncovered an old towel, which she spread in its bottom. This would be perfect; shallow enough for the mother cat to get in and out but deep enough so the kittens couldn't, at least for a day or two.

Skye and Jermer were getting the two kittens settled in the box when the mother cat came back with a third, which she dropped into Skye's outstretched hand.

This one was bigger than the other two, a husky male, mostly black but with a white mask and white legs partway up as if he were wearing a black sweater with pushed-up sleeves.

"That one's Floyd," Jermer said, picking up the kitten.

"Why Floyd?" Skye asked. "Does he remind you of somebody?"

Jermer's forehead wrinkled as he looked into the placid, little cat face. "I'm not sure. I think I remember a cat named Floyd up by the Snake River."

"What were you doing by the Snake River?" Skye asked.

Jermer shook his head. "I think I used to live there with my dad. That was before I came to live with Sweetie."

Skye didn't know a lot about Jermer. All Sweetie had told her was that his mother had died when he was born, and that she'd got him when he was four. She hadn't said where from or why. Skye wished now that she'd asked Sweetie more about him.

"Floyd it is," Skye said. "And I hope he's the last kitten."

Apparently he was because the mother cat, wetter and more bedraggled than ever now, lay down on the floor to watch Skye and Jermer. She looked exhausted.

"Now maybe she'll eat," Skye said, carefully giving Floyd to Jermer and walking over to the refrigerator. "I'll get her some of the meat left over from the wedding. She's so skinny. Come on, babe."

Jermer scooted himself along the floor to the cat's side, still holding Floyd. "Babe," he said. "Babe."

Okay, so the mother cat was Babe. Now all the cats had names.

Babe got to her feet as soon as Skye opened the refrigerator. She came over to wind herself through Skye's legs, meowing politely but urgently.

Skye was pulling scraps of meat from a hambone when Grandpa came back from the barn. He came in unzipping his jacket and shaking the rain from it. "Right wet outside," he said, then stopped, looking at Babe and the box of kittens. "What's this, Sis?"

Something in his voice made Skye's stomach twist.

"Remember the cat I asked about at breakfast?" she said quickly. "The one you said was a stray? She just moved in with her babies."

Grandpa zipped his jacket up again. "Well, we better move her right back out again before she gets settled in. Don't feed her, or we'll never get rid of her."

Without even waiting for Skye to tell about her plans for the kittens, he took Floyd from Jermer and deposited him in the box with the other two kittens. Then he picked the box up and headed for the door. The kittens skidded around inside, mewing for their mother. Babe loped along at Grandpa's feet, yowling with alarm.

Jermer got up, grabbing his umbrella and backpack and boxes. "I guess we won't be playing games," he said.

"Grandpa," Skye wailed, running after him. "Let me keep them. We've already named them. The mother is Babe and the little ones are Floyd and Oh and Twinkie."

Grandpa walked right on out of the door into the rain. "You should never give a name to something you can't keep, Sis," he said. "Don't set yourself up for sorrow."

"Grandpa," Skye wailed again. "Grandpa, I *am*

going to keep one of the kittens. Reanna will let me take one. Just one."

"Wouldn't count on it, Sis." Grandpa kept walking.

"I'll find homes for the others," Skye pleaded. "The aunts. The cousins. Somebody will want them."

What was the use? Why hadn't she just gone with Mr. Jensen that morning? By now she would have been sitting happily in Reanna and Bill's tent, telling them how she'd managed to find them. Reanna would be saying how proud she was that she had such a resourceful daughter, and Bill. . . . Well, who cared what Bill thought? She'd be there, and he'd just have to put up with her, like it or not.

She should have gone. The kittens were going to die anyway.

This time she didn't have to try to cry because the tears, hot and stinging, streamed down her face and fell along with the rain onto the skinny cat at her feet. "Grandpa," she cried.

As if things weren't bad enough, Aunt Esta's car drove into the yard just then and came to a careful stop in the rain-slicked mud. Aunt Esta peered out, and so did someone in the backseat. Denise, it was, and Lee Esther, too, on the other side.

They stared out at Skye who stood there bawling in the rain. The last time they'd seen her, when Reanna and Bill left, she'd been blubbering, too. They probably thought that's all she ever did.

Skye saw them look at one another and smile.

SEVEN

AUNT ESTA GOT OUT OF THE CAR. SHE WAS dressed in an aqua-colored pantsuit with an apron over it, as if she'd just taken a few minutes away from her kitchen duties. She held a plastic bag over her neat gray hair to keep the rain off.

Lee Esther and Denise got out, too, and just then Tarzan came bounding around the corner of the barn, probably wanting to see who was there.

First he ran toward the cousins, tail whirling in excitement. Then he spotted the mother cat, who was practically crawling up Grandpa's leg trying to get to her mewing kittens in the box. Abruptly he changed directions and came toward the cat, barking instructions to get off his turf.

Babe, skinny as a coat hanger, stood her ground, arching her back and ballooning her tail.

Skye flapped her arms at Tarzan, screaming, "Go away! Go away!"

Jermer charged at him, too, but slipped in the mud and went down, his armful of games flying. One of the smaller boxes came open and spilled cards all over the oozy yard.

Even Grandpa shooed at Tarzan, swinging the kitten box awkwardly, which caused the frightened kittens to cry louder.

Babe hissed and yowled, flashing her claws as she leaped at Tarzan. He barked at her, stepping back when she slashed out and made a bloody scratch down the length of his snout. Yelping, he headed back to the barn.

Inside the box, the kittens wailed.

Skye tried to pick the mother cat up, but she snarled and raised a clawed paw.

"Leave her alone for a spell," Aunt Esta called. "She'll calm down if you give her time."

Skye backed away, trembling.

Jermer picked himself up and surveyed his muddy games. "My Uno's ruined," he said, pulling a dripping card from a puddle of rainwater.

Denise and Lee Esther stood like soggy, silent statues, watching.

From the shelter of her plastic bag, Aunt Esta demanded, "What's going on here? Orville, what have you got in that box?"

"Cats," Grandpa said. "Just taking them back to the barn where they belong."

"They're like to get torn apart out there, if that fool dog has his say." Aunt Esta turned to Skye and opened her mouth again, then closed it.

Knowing everybody was looking at her, Skye tried to stop her dumb crying. She knew her nose was running, but she didn't have a tissue or hanky she could wipe it on. She scrubbed her sleeve across it, realizing that wasn't the kind of thing you ought to do in front of somebody like Aunt Esta.

But all Aunt Esta did was sigh as she tucked her plastic bag under her arm and reached in the pocket of her apron for a lace-edged handkerchief, which she handed to Skye. It smelled like rose petals.

"Blow," Aunt Esta said and waited for Skye to do so. Taking the slimy hanky and stowing it back in her pocket, she said, "You're bawling about cats?"

Skye glared at her as belligerently as she could through watery eyes. "They're not just cats. They've got names. I'm bawling about Floyd and Oh and Twinkie. And Babe." She pointed at the mother cat who patroled the area, her tail still puffed up to twice its size. "You'd bawl, too, if somebody was taking away the only pets you'd ever had."

"Mouthy," Aunt Esta said. "Just like your mother."

Skye sucked in air to say more, but Aunt Esta held up a hand. "My stars, Orville," she said, "let the girl have the cats. It's a hard enough time for her. Let her have them while she's here."

Totally surprised by Aunt Esta's unexpected understanding, Skye leaked fresh tears, hunching over with embarrassment to hide them.

One of the cousins snickered. Skye couldn't tell whether it was Denise or Lee Esther.

Grandpa muttered something about not being able to take care of *all* the animals that people threw away, but Aunt Esta marched over to him and took the box of kittens.

"Here," she said, depositing it in Skye's arms. "You're responsible for them while you're here and responsible for getting rid of them when you leave. All right?"

Skye checked the wet kittens, then nodded toward Babe. "Her, too. She's hungry, and the kittens need her."

"She'll come when you take the kittens inside," Aunt Esta said. "Don't worry about her. It appears to me she can take care of herself."

Clutching the box of kittens, Skye started toward the house, avoiding looking at Aunt Esta or the cousins. Sure enough, Babe followed her.

"Your Grandma Abby didn't take to having animals inside, Sis," Grandpa protested. "She always kept cats outdoors. She'd throw a fit if she knew her house would be crawling with cats."

"Abby's dead," Aunt Esta said, as if that ended the discussion. "Skye, hold your horses a minute. Wait till I have a chance to say a word to you.

A bunch of us will be coming here tomorrow to houseclean, and I expect you to be available to help."

She turned to Grandpa. "I came over to find out what cleaning equipment you haven't thrown out since Abby died."

"Ding, ding, ding," Grandpa said.

Skye stopped, hitching up a shoulder to wipe her nose, which was running again. "The house is already clean. Grandpa keeps it real clean." She shifted the box of kittens awkwardly.

Aunt Esta came over, lifted up the hem of her apron and wiped Skye's face with it, the way you would do to a little kid. Skye hoped Denise and Lee Esther had suddenly gone blind so they hadn't seen it.

"Let me tell you about this house," Aunt Esta said. "My grandfather — who was your grandpa's grandfather, too, and Belva's and Vernell's — built this house. You're the fifth generation to call it home."

Skye opened her mouth to say that she did *not* call it home, but Aunt Esta went right on.

"Our father was born here. Your grandpa and I, and Belva and Vernell, were born here. Your grandpa brought your Grandma Abby here as a bride, and your mother was born here, and you, too, for that matter."

Skye knew she'd been born there, but it had never been home.

Aunt Esta was still talking. "This house is part of all of us. Every summer since it was built it's been gone through, top to bottom, every inch of it scrubbed and dusted and polished. Your grandma Abby up and died and now your grandpa doesn't care whether it falls down around his ears, but I'm going to do right by this house every summer until I'm all too old to hold a scrub brush. Heaven knows it should have been cleaned before Reanna's wedding, but she didn't let us know but a week ahead of time."

Aunt Esta gave a gusty sigh. "We'll be here at eight o'clock in the morning, so be up and ready."

There wasn't much else to say but, "Yes, ma'am." Skye couldn't leave anyway until she'd found homes for the kittens. "I'll help if you'll show me how," she added.

"All I can say is it's a good thing you finally got away from that flighty mother of yours long enough to learn a thing or two," Aunt Esta said.

"Yes, ma'am," Skye said again. It annoyed her to have Aunt Esta talk that way about Reanna. But after all, it was Aunt Esta who saved the kittens, so Skye figured the least she could do was be nice.

She started toward the house again, and Aunt Esta followed, saying she'd check in the cellar to see if there were buckets and mops there. "Denise and Lee Esther will be coming back tomorrow, too," she said. "Maybe you'll be in more of a mood to talk to them then. You can ask your little friend if he'd like to help, if you want, but you'd best get Sweetie's permission first."

Skye's face flushed. That was the final humiliation, to be paired with Jermer as if she'd not want to do anything without him. That was just one more thing Lee Esther and Denise would be blabbing to the rest of the Cousins by the Dozens, along with what a crybaby Skye had been about the kittens.

After Aunt Esta and the cousins left, Grandpa apologized for trying to get rid of the kittens. "Didn't realize you set such store by them, Sis. Guess it's okay for you to have them until they're old enough to give away, but make dang sure you clean up after them."

"Thanks, Grandpa," Skye said as he went back to the barn.

Jermer helped Skye dry off the kittens, mourning all the while for his rain-soaked games. After she fed Babe, Skye got some rags to wipe the mud off some of the games. But the Uno cards were hopeless. Jermer put them into a plastic bag that he carried with him when he and Skye walked over to Sweetie's house to ask if he could help houseclean the next day.

They left Babe and the kittens fast asleep in the warm box in a corner of the kitchen with the door closed. Since both Grandpa and Tarzan were back at the barn, Skye felt she could leave the little family for a while.

It would have been easier just to call Sweetie, but there was one problem. Sweetie didn't have a telephone. Skye didn't know why that was. She'd asked Jermer once, but he'd shrugged and said they didn't need one because nobody ever called them anyway. Skye had asked how could anybody call them if they didn't have a telephone, but Jermer had just shrugged again. It was another thing she'd have to ask Sweetie about sometime, and maybe about the little log cabin she and Jermer lived in that looked as if it were as old as the hills behind it.

Sweetie was just taking fresh bread from the oven of her old wood-burning stove when Skye and Jermer got to her house. Today she was dressed in her usual faded jeans and oversized shirt. Her hair was pulled back and tied up with a blue bandanna.

"Sit down," she said after she'd clucked over Jermer's ruined cards. "Eat." She sawed away at one of the fresh loaves with a big knife.

The smell of the bread made Skye's stomach growl. She could stay long enough to eat. The kittens were all right for now. Besides, she liked Sweetie's house a lot. A telephone wasn't the only thing Sweetie didn't have. She also didn't have a television or even electric lights, although there were wires coming to her house from the utility poles along the road. For light she used a couple of old kerosene lamps she said had belonged to her grandmother. She had one of them lit now, sitting in the middle of her big round oak table since the rain made the day gloomy. In the lamplight the room looked cozy and friendly.

The thick bread, dripping with Sweetie's homemade butter, was good and warm and comforting. Skye relaxed as she ate at the big table with Sweetie and Jermer. She found herself telling about the kittens and how they'd been saved and that she'd promised to be responsible for them.

"I love them, Sweetie," she said. "They're so little and helpless." She told about Floyd, how husky he was, and Twinkie, the way she was so sassy and hissed even though she was no bigger than a thumb, and Oh, who looked as if he were wearing overalls.

"Ah," Sweetie crooned. "So many soft, sweet things that need to be taken care of."

Skye took another bite of the warm bread. "It's going to be hard to give any of them away. Sweetie, how soon can kittens leave their mother? I think they're close to a month old now."

"They have to be weaned and big enough to take care of themselves," Sweetie said. "Six weeks at the very least. You'll be in school by the time they're old enough. Maybe some of your classmates would like a kitten or two. And speaking of school, somebody needs to get you registered."

Skye shook her head. "I won't be here for school. Reanna and Bill are coming back for me."

Sweetie looked at her for so long that Skye became uneasy. Then Sweetie said, "Hasn't your grandpa given you the letter Reanna left for you?"

"Letter? No, he hasn't given me any letter." The uneasiness increased. "What letter?"

Sweetie bustled over to the counter where she began sawing more bread from the still-steaming loaf. "Here, I'll give you a hunk to take home with you. When you get there, you tell your grandpa it's high time you saw that letter. He should have given it to you last night."

"Can you stay for the funeral?" Jermer asked.

Something big and hard was lodged in Skye's chest. She put down the rest of her piece of bread. She couldn't swallow past that lump. "What funeral?" she asked.

"For my Uno cards," Jermer said. "I'm going to bury them."

Skye nodded. She'd stay. Why would she want to hurry back to Grandpa's house? From the look on Sweetie's face, that letter could only be bad news.

EIGHT

GRANDPA WASN'T HOME WHEN SKYE GOT there. Not in the house where the old kitchen clock tocked softly to itself, nor in the barn where his gray horse lopped its ears forward and whickered at her. The red farm truck was gone and so was Tarzan.

Maybe Grandpa'd left a note, a few scribbled words to let her know where he'd gone. Skye checked the hopeless jumble of magazines and old mail that sat on and fell off of the telephone desk. If she should just happen to find the letter from Reanna, if it should just show up there in the pile, it wouldn't hurt to open it, would it? Sweetie'd said Reanna had left it for *her*.

There was a stack of *Reader's Digest*s and a lot of receipts for bills Grandpa'd paid, but no note from him. No letter from Reanna, either.

Disappointed, Skye sat on the floor next to the kittens' pasteboard house and watched them for a while, trying not to think about the letter and what it might say.

The kittens were all awake now, spiky little tails aloft, bright eyes alert. They raced around their small home, tumbling over their own feet, leaping at one another, occasionally standing on their hind legs to try to reach the top of the box. It was obvious they wanted their freedom, and it wouldn't be long until they could get out on their own.

Babe was there in the box, too, trying to stage a lick-in. She lay on her side, hanging out her tongue to lick whoever happened to come by. She was purring, and Skye got a whole lot of satisfaction from knowing that for the first time in days, maybe months, the cat wasn't hungry.

But Skye couldn't keep her thoughts from going back to that letter. Probably Grandpa had it stashed somewhere in his bedroom. Why hadn't he given it to her?

Would it be snooping if she went to his bedroom to look for a letter that rightfully belonged to her? Maybe Grandpa had even left a note in there.

Without letting herself think a whole lot about it, Skye went into Grandpa's bedroom, which was on the ground floor across the hall from the kitchen, and stood there looking around.

Grandpa kept the room just as it was when Grandma was alive. He made the bed carefully each morning with the family history quilt Grandma had made. Skye liked the pretty quilt. On each block Grandma had stitched some part of her life, cut out of calico or some other bright cloth. A narrow house made of white material and trimmed with gingham decorated one block. On another was a wedding bouquet that was supposed to be like the one Grandma Abby had carried as a bride.

On a block near the center of the quilt was the figure of a girl with brown hair. That was Reanna, and a smaller figure with brown braids and blue eyes was a likeness of Skye at age three. Even Tarzan was on that quilt.

There were blue curtains at the bedroom windows, and on the wall where you could see it from the bed was a picture of a girl in an old-fashioned dress, standing by some tall red hollyhocks.

It was the kind of room that invited you to stay.

But Skye was there to look for a letter.

Without touching anything, she looked on all the surfaces in the room, resisting the temptation to open drawers. That would be snooping by anybody's definition, and she wasn't a snoop. Not that much, anyway.

She didn't find what she was looking for, but in the painted metal box on Grandpa's dresser was something better. There among a handful of coins and some stray bolts and nails were the keys to Reanna's car.

Skye picked them up, holding them in her hand, running a finger along their rough edges. Here was her freedom. Reanna had never let her drive anywhere but in empty parking lots, but would it be any different on the empty roads of Sheep Creek? At night there wasn't any traffic to speak of, and that campground where Reanna and Bill would surely be wasn't very far away.

Skye was so happy she did a little dance across the room and fell right onto Grandma's family quilt on the bed, kicking her feet in the air and laughing aloud. She hoped snippy Denise and Lee Esther wouldn't suddenly pop in while she was being crazy.

She was still lying there on the quilt when she heard Grandpa's truck in the yard. Putting the keys back into the painted box, Skye hurried to the kitchen and was sitting on the floor watching the kittens when Grandpa came in.

He was apologetic. "Sorry, Sis. Had to go borrow some tools. Thought I'd be home before you got back from Sweetie's." He washed his hands at the kitchen sink. "I'll hustle now and fix us some grub."

"Sweetie sent bread." Skye pointed at the plastic-wrapped package on the counter.

"Right nice of her," Grandpa said. "It'll go good with what we're having."

"Grandpa," Skye began. She wasn't quite sure how to ask about the letter except to just plunge right in. "Sweetie said Reanna left something for me."

"Not now, Sis." Grandpa dried his hands on the spotless dish towel Aunt Esta had put there just before the wedding. "I need a bite to eat before I talk about anything Sweetie said."

Skye didn't see why he couldn't talk and fix the noonday dinner at the same time. She bit her tongue to keep from blurting out a demand to see the letter *right now*, which would sound pretty babyish and besides, she had the idea Grandpa wouldn't take to that kind of sass any more than Aunt Esta would. She'd just have to wait and ease into the subject gradually.

She watched while he sliced potatoes into a grease-filled frying pan. When he got a couple of eggs from the refrigerator and broke them over the potatoes, she wished she'd fixed the midday dinner herself. She could have done a salad from the stuff left in Grandpa's garden and then made Tuna Surprise, which was a can of tuna fish mixed in with some cooked noodles and a can of mushroom soup, then a few little marshmallows sprinkled on top. It was another of Reanna's great recipes.

Skye didn't say anything while Grandpa stirred the mess in the frying pan and dumped it out on two plates. The eggs made a slimy coating on the potatoes, but she picked up her fork and began to eat.

Grandpa was silent as they ate, leaning his arms against the edge of the table and hunching over his food.

Skye cleared her throat. "Grandpa, what was Reanna like when she was my age?" That was as good a place to start as any.

He glanced up at her. "Danged if I know, Sis. She lived here and growed up right in this house, but danged if I ever knew what she was like. Used to say she'd stifle if she had to stay here a minute longer. Didn't like the farm, didn't like the mountains, didn't like the town. A prison, she called it. Her ma and I, we tried every which way to make her happy. But she didn't want any of it. Took off and got married to your dad the very night she graduated from high school. That lasted a year, just long enough to get you birthed."

It was the longest speech Skye had ever heard him make. The most interesting part to Skye was the mention of her father. Reanna wouldn't talk about him. Skye knew his name — Scott McCabe — and that he'd been tall and brown-haired, but that was about all the information she had. She'd got some birthday cards from him when she was little, but Reanna hadn't let her send anything back to him, even her address. That wouldn't have done much good anyway, since they moved so often.

"My dad," Skye said. "Grandpa, what was *he* like?"

Grandpa speared a hunk of fried potato with his fork. "Nice enough young fella. Liked to dance and run around in that red convertible he had. Snappiest car in town, which is probably what caught Reanna's eye. She climbed into it with him on the night she graduated and rolled right out of here."

He put the hunk of potato into his mouth and chewed, indicating he'd said all he was going to, which was just as well since Skye didn't especially like what he was saying about Reanna. If Scott McCabe was so nice, maybe *that* was what attracted Reanna to him, not just his flashy car. And if he really was such a nice young fella, why had he up and left the two of them alone?

Or was it Reanna who'd left him alone?

Skye poked at her food. Now that Grandpa'd had a bite or two, maybe he'd answer her question. "Grandpa, what Sweetie said Reanna left for me was a letter."

"Sweetie'd ought to keep her mouth shut," Grandpa said. He went on chewing.

"I'd like to see the letter, Grandpa."

"I'll tell you what's in it when you need to know." He didn't even look up this time.

"I need to know *now*."

"Not now, Sis. Wait a day or two."

"It's *my* letter," Skye said. "Reanna left it for

78

me. You have no right to keep it from me."

Now Grandpa did look up, his face reddening. "Man who's been around as long as I have ought to know more than a twit of a girl. You're better off not seeing that letter right now. Settle in for a few days with them cats, then I'll show it to you."

Skye could feel her own face reddening. "So how am I going to think of anything else while I sit around and wait for your few days to pass? If Reanna left a letter for me, she must have meant for me to read it."

Grandpa gazed at her, his fist planted firmly on the table with his fork sprouting up out of it. "You're just like her. Strong-headed and stubborn."

"How about mouthy?" Skye shrilled. "Aunt Esta said I was mouthy like Reanna."

Grandpa nodded. "That, too."

Skye stood up. "Doesn't anybody have anything good to say about Reanna? No wonder she got out of here, if everybody thought she was so awful."

Slowly the redness faded from Grandpa's face. "I'm sorry, Sis," he said. "I got a-goin' there with you the same as I used to do with her. Didn't mean to do that." He laid his fork down and put both hands flat on the table. "There's a lot of good to Reanna. Hard worker, she is, when she wants to be. Smart, too. We loved her, Sis. Her ma and I. Didn't understand her much, but we loved her."

He looked at his plate, then picked up a piece of Sweetie's bread and sopped up what was left of his quivery egg. "Reanna did leave a letter for you. Said I was to give it to you only if you didn't take to the idea of staying here. I thought maybe you'd get so interested in them cats that you'd decide on your own to . . ."

He didn't finish saying what he thought she'd decide to do. Shoving the dripping piece of bread into his mouth, he pushed his chair back and got up, heading for the bedroom.

Skye sat down, knowing now more than ever that she had to get out of there as soon as she could, the same as Reanna had done.

NINE

FROM THE BEDROOM SKYE HEARD THE JANGLE of keys. Had she left some clue that she'd found Reanna's car keys? Was Grandpa hiding them so she couldn't get them? Did he suspect what she had in mind?

By leaning far to her left she could see across the hall and into the bedroom. Grandpa was down on his knees beside the bed, pulling something from under it. Skye hadn't thought to look there when she was scouting the room.

The keys jangled again, and Skye knew Grandpa'd had the letter locked up. Suddenly she wished she'd never asked about it. Most likely it was just a list of shoulds and oughts that Reanna didn't want her to forget. But why would Grandpa lock up something like that?

He brought the letter to her. It was addressed to Skye, and in Reanna's backslanted handwriting it said:

81

Dearest Skye,

You know how bad I am at saying what's in my heart. I'm hoping I can tell you what I need to say before Bill and I go, but just in case I can't, I'm leaving this letter.

Skye didn't want to read any further, but the words were there and she couldn't take her eyes from them. She read on.

Skye, honeybun, Bill and I are going to be gone for an entire year doing research for the book I told you about. We'll be moving from one place to another every week or so. As you can see, that wouldn't be very good for your school attendance.

Who cared about school? So she'd miss it for a year. Skye read on.

That's why we're leaving you with Grandpa and the family for a year. You'll like it there, Skye. If I didn't truly think you would, I couldn't leave you. Give it a chance.

The letter was signed: *Lots of love, Reanna.*

Lots of love. If Reanna loved her even a little bit, she wouldn't be abandoning her there in the place she herself had hated. Maybe it hadn't been Bill's idea. Maybe Reanna had thought it up herself. Maybe she'd got tired of dragging Skye around with her. Maybe she was ashamed of having such a big daughter, who made her seem older than she wanted to be.

Skye could feel Grandpa watching her. Carefully she tore the letter into strips, then shredded the strips, creating a handful of confetti that she dropped into the grease left on her plate.

"I'm sorry, Sis," Grandpa said. "Your ma, she just couldn't bring herself to tell you. Never was one to face up to things. Wasn't too happy about leaving you, but the aunts put on a lot of pressure about you needing some place to call home and some decent schooling. Reanna can't seem to stay put in any one place. Then there was the thing about her and that new man of hers needing some time by themselves." Grandpa sagged from the ordeal of a second long speech, but he reached over awkwardly to pat her shoulder. "Heck of a note. She thought you might just settle right in and want to stay. If Sweetie'd kept her mouth shut, maybe you would of."

If Sweetie'd kept her mouth shut, Skye would have gone on from one day to the next thinking Reanna was coming back to get her any minute. By the end of a year her mind would have been as shredded as the letter she'd just torn up.

How could any of them think she could live there with Grandpa, who hadn't even understood his own child, much less his grandchild?

Skye knew exactly what she was going to do. She'd leave that very night, after Grandpa'd gone to bed. She'd take the box of cats with her in the station wagon. When she found Reanna and Bill she'd tell them she was keeping all the kittens and if they objected she'd turn them in for abandoning a child. That had happened on one of the TV shows she and Reanna watched.

She worried momentarily about gas. Reanna always ran on the bottom half of the tank because of never having enough money to fill it up.

But surely what was in the car would take Skye as far as that campground on the riverbank where Reanna and Bill would be.

Satisfied with her reasoning, Skye relaxed. All she had to do now was wait for Grandpa to go to sleep.

She kept herself busy all through the late afternoon and early evening washing dishes and tidying up the house. She checked the map Bill had given her, trying to remember which was the right road to take to the campground. It looked simple enough on the map. But all those confusing valleys and little unidentified roads bothered her.

What if Reanna and Bill had already gone on? Then which way should Skye turn when she got to Preston? There were roads on the map going in every direction from there.

She'd just count on them being at the campground by the river. The important thing was to get going.

After supper, which was just bread and milk and cheese, Skye went through all the stuff that overflowed the telephone desk. She made a stack of the old magazines to go to the aunts or whoever wanted them. She filed the receipts carefully in a box she found. The advertisements she threw away.

She liked to leave a place better than she'd found it. That's what she and Reanna had always done.

Of course that night had to be one of the times when Grandpa stayed up forever. He puttered around until time for the late news, then sat down to watch and even snored a while during the sports events.

Skye kept sneaking downstairs to check things out. One of the times she was down there she tiptoed into Grandpa's bedroom and got the car keys from his painted box, easing them out carefully so they wouldn't jangle and wake him. She stowed them in a pocket of her jeans, wrapping them first in a tissue to keep them quiet as she moved around.

Her duffel was all packed, and she'd prepared a bag of scraps for Babe as well as some canned stuff and crackers for herself.

The last thing to do was to write Grandpa a note.

She didn't say much. He'd probably be relieved that she'd gone. She started out with *Dear Grandpa,* and then just said, *I've gone to find Reanna. I can't stay here a whole year.* She signed it, *Your granddaughter, Skye.*

She folded the note, wrote *Grandpa* on it, and left it by the box of Wheaties on the kitchen table.

She worried a little about what she'd do for money if she didn't find Reanna and Bill right off. The food she was taking with her wasn't going to last forever, and then there was gas to buy.

But she had almost ten dollars, and even if Reanna and Bill weren't at the campground, they couldn't have gone farther than one tank of gas would take her, not with the rain and all.

Finally, right after the old kitchen clock had struck twelve, the TV went off and Skye heard Grandpa's footsteps going into the bedroom. It wasn't long before the snoring started up again. Enough to rattle the windowpanes, Grandpa's snoring was. He wasn't going to wake up even when she started the car motor.

Skye hurried downstairs with her duffel, taking it right out to the station wagon and putting it where it was handy. Tarzan barked at her, but she shushed him with a few words. He came over to see what she was doing, tail wagging, poking his big nose inside the car and sniffing at the duffel. Skye put him on his chain that was fastened to the yardlight pole, promising she'd let him go before she left for good.

She packed the food bags and a litter box for Babe and filled a quart jar with water and put that in the back of the car. Reanna'd always said you should never go anywhere without water.

Last of all, she carried out the box of kittens. They were asleep in a furry lump in one corner and didn't wake up even when Skye touched their warm little bodies.

Babe, who didn't take to being carried, followed along at Skye's feet, worrying about her babies, hissing at Tarzan who barked at her from his chain, fussing about the interruption to her night's sleep. She didn't want to get into the station wagon. She eyed it suspiciously, yowling when Skye picked her up and put her inside.

So now everything was ready to go. The rain had slowed down to a mere drizzle, so Skye would be able to see all right. Everything was working out just fine.

Except that the car wouldn't start. When Skye turned the key, all it did was give out a sick-sounding *r-r-r-r-r*, then even that died away, and the only sounds in the night were the crickets singing and Babe yowling and Tarzan whining because Skye had forgotten to let him off his chain.

Ten

SKYE SAT FOR A LONG TIME THERE IN THE DEAD car, staring out at the dripping cottonwoods. Reanna always said nothing mattered as much as freedom. She said money, nice clothes, fancy houses, nothing was important if you weren't free.

Skye was trapped as surely as if someone had tied her to the yardlight pole, the way she'd done to Tarzan.

In the back of the car Babe pawed frantically at the windows, howling to be let out. The kittens woke up. Hearing their mother's panic, they cried and scrambled around in their pasteboard prison.

What was there to do but take them all back into the house and try to get them calmed down? Skye wasn't going anywhere, not that night.

After she got the cats settled she tore up the note she'd written for Grandpa, then went upstairs. But instead of going to bed, she unfolded her map and studied it again, while the old house snapped and creaked around her. Which way would Bill and Reanna go when they left their campground? How was Skye going to find them now?

The old kitchen clock struck three in the silence of the night before her eyes would no longer see the words on the map, and she slept.

Jermer awakened her. From the bottom of the stairs he yelled, "Skye. Skye. It's time to get up."

What was he doing there in the middle of the night?

When Skye managed to drag one eye open she saw that it was no longer night. In fact, her bedside clock said five minutes before eight.

"Skye," Jermer bayed.

Didn't the kid ever stay home? Didn't Sweetie have things for him to do at her house, especially when people wanted to sleep?

"Skye," he yelled again. "Aunt Esta will be here soon."

The housecleaning! Skye'd totally forgotten about that.

She got up and dressed quickly. It wouldn't do to be lolling in bed when Aunt Esta came. And Denise and Lee Esther — they'd probably be coming, and if they caught her in her pajamas she'd never hear the end of it. Why hadn't Grandpa awakened her?

Grandpa wasn't anywhere to be seen when she

got downstairs, but Jermer was sitting by the kitten box, his blue backpack beside him.

"Oh wants to get out," he said. He pointed at little Oh who leaped up far enough to hook his front paws over the edge of the box but then couldn't hoist himself the rest of the way out.

Skye reached down and scooped Oh out, depositing him on the floor. Spiky little tail up, he ran across the kitchen. "He wants to go somewhere," she said, not adding that she knew how he felt. Yawning from lack of sleep, she walked over to the refrigerator where Babe sat, politely waiting for breakfast.

Jermer followed the kitten, scooting along on his seat. "Me, too," he said. "I want to go somewhere."

That surprised Skye. She would have said Jermer was perfectly content at Sweetie's place. But then why did he always carry that backpack with him?

"Where is it you want to go?"

Jermer's face took on the puzzled look that was becoming familiar to Skye. "I'm not real sure. The Snake River, I think."

She remembered that he'd talked about the Snake River before. "Why do you want to go there, Jermer?"

His forehead furrowed again. "I guess I forgot why."

Opening the refrigerator door, Skye found

90

some scraps for Babe, then went to the table and poured herself some Crispy Critters. "I've been wondering about your backpack," she said. "What is it you've got in there?"

"Things I need when I go," Jermer said. "Peanut butter. Some boiled eggs. Things." He turned back to the window and announced, "Aunt Esta's car is here. And another one. Lots of people are coming."

Skye poured the Crispy Critters back into the box. She wasn't going to be sitting there eating little kid cereal when the cousins came in. If she got too hungry before lunch, she'd borrow one of those boiled eggs Jermer had in his backpack.

"Orville?" Aunt Esta bellowed as she barged into the house like a general with her small army in tow. "Orville, we're going to need your help today."

"Grandpa's not here," Skye said, realizing why Grandpa had disappeared. "His truck is gone, and Tarzan, too."

Aunt Esta sighed. "Just like him to run off." She set down the basket she carried, full of small pails, scrub brushes, rags, and a big bottle of Mr. Clean. "Well, we'll just have to do things our own way."

Skye had a feeling that would have been the case even if Grandpa'd been there.

Aunt Belva was among the people who'd just arrived, and she came over to hug Skye, asking how she was. Aunt Belva wasn't a talker like Aunt Esta, and she was likely to fade away to non-existence when Aunt Esta was around. Skye liked her.

"I'm fine, Aunt Belva," she said.

Aunt Belva looked closely at her. "Are you really, honey?"

Her face was so concerned that Skye wanted to drag her off to a corner where she could unload all her problems about wanting to be with Reanna and about Grandpa not understanding her a bit. But Aunt Esta marched over and said, "Come on, Belva. Let's go on down to the cellar and get what little stuff Orville kept. My stars, you'd think when he gets an attack of the neats, he'd keep useful things like brooms and rags. Why, Abby always kept a good pile of cleaning supplies." Still talking, she headed down the cellar stairs.

Behind her back, Aunt Belva shrugged as she gave Skye a smile, then followed Aunt Esta.

Suddenly a kitten mewed frantically. Skye looked around, alarmed. She'd forgotten to put Oh back in the box. Had someone stepped on him?

No. Denise was holding him up by the scruff of his little neck. "Look what I found," she said.

Skye leaped at her. "Put him down," she demanded, then, making her voice calmer she said, "Let me have him. He's scared."

Denise held him high over her head. He mewed louder. "What's his name?"

Skye swallowed. "His name is Oh." Her voice came out high and babyish.

"Oh?" Denise said with a grin toward Lee Esther. "And how is it you spell that?"

Skye tried to stay calm. "Just plain O–H. May I have him now, please, Denise? He's mine."

"He's just a stray," Denise said. "I can do anything I want with him."

Skye reached for the kitten. She wasn't going to bawl this time. That's what Denise wanted, for her to blubber like a baby right in front of all the other cousins. Skye wasn't going to do that.

But Oh mewed again and she could feel the dumb tears filling her eyes. She knew Denise saw because she smiled and held the kitten up higher.

"Please," Skye said.

"Cool it, Denise." Cody, the tall guy-cousin, had just come into the house. He spoke sharply to Denise. "Do what Skye says."

"I wasn't going to hurt the stupid cat," Denise said. "I found the dumb thing on the floor."

"Put him in the box with the other kittens," Cody insisted.

Denise glared at him. "Whose boss are you?"

But the funny thing was, she did as Cody said. Denise, Miss Queen-of-the-World Denise, obeyed her brother, putting Oh in the box with the other kittens. Then she stomped across the room to whisper to Lee Esther.

Skye quickly scrubbed the tears from her eyes before she gave Cody a grateful look.

The other cousins gathered around the box to look at the kittens and reach down to pet them. Skye watched anxiously. There were four cousins besides Denise and Lee Esther and Cody, a teen-aged girl named Junie and another whose name Skye couldn't recall, as well as two boys who were nine or ten years old.

None of the mothers were there. Some of them had jobs in Preston, Skye knew, and a couple of them were busy with new babies. The fathers of the cousins and the husbands of the aunts were doing their farming chores, Skye figured. She wondered why Cody wasn't off with them instead of here to do housecleaning.

Cody came over to Skye. "Denise likes to aggravate people," he said.

"I noticed that," she said, and Cody grinned.

"She's my sister, you know," he said.

Skye knew that, but she hadn't sorted out which families all the other cousins belonged to yet. Lee Esther, she knew, was one of Aunt Esta's grandchildren. Skye had figured that out mainly because she'd heard Lee Esther call Aunt Esta "Grandma."

"Are you and Denise Aunt Esta's grandkids?" Skye asked.

Cody rolled his eyes as he shook his head. "Belva is our grandma," he said. "Thank goodness," he added, which made Skye grin.

You could never tell how people were going to turn out, she thought. Aunt Belva was as nice as anybody Skye'd ever met, but Denise hadn't inherited any of it, although Cody had. Skye's own grandma had been a home-loving soul, but Reanna'd turned her back on all that kind of thing.

Aunt Esta and Aunt Belva came back from the cellar, interrupting Skye's thoughts. "All right, all right, let's get on with it," Aunt Esta said. "It's too drizzly to take the bedding out to air, so today we'll concentrate on cleaning the walls and floors and closets, both upstairs and down."

She made assignments. "Belva, you take Lee Esther and Denise and Skye upstairs and get started there. Junie and Lisa and you boys, you stay here with me and we'll do the kitchen and dining room."

Aunt Esta said "you boys" as if she couldn't remember their names any more than Skye could.

She wasn't finished. "Cody," she said, "you start in the parlor. Get the furniture moved to the center of the room and start cleaning the walls and ceiling. You'll need the ladder."

Now Skye knew why Cody was there rather than out in the fields. Aunt Esta needed some muscle, and apparently Cody was elected to provide it. You didn't argue with Aunt Esta.

"What about me?" Jermer asked. "What should I do?"

"I'll need help in the parlor," Cody said. "Some really good workers. I'll need Jermer."

That was nice of him, Skye thought. It made Jermer grin proudly.

"And Skye," Cody said. "I'll need you, too."

Skye could feel her face flush. Was he choosing her so she'd feel better about making a fool of herself bawling over the kittens? If he was, he could just forget it. She wasn't going to work with anybody who felt sorry for her.

Denise put her hands on her hips. "How come I have to go up and clean Skye's room while she gets to stay down here?"

Skye changed her mind. "I'll help you, Cody." If it bent Denise out of shape, then she wanted to do it.

"Aunt Esta," Denise said. "I want to work in the parlor."

"Do as you're told," Aunt Esta said. "Now let's get to it."

Denise turned and followed the others, but she and Lee Esther meowed as they went upstairs, just to remind Skye what a baby she was.

So who cared? Who needed cousins anyway?

Cody motioned for Skye and Jermer to head for the parlor and he followed behind them, humming and doing something with his nose, making a sound something like bagpipes. Stopping in the doorway, he whispered, "If anybody tries to come in, we'll cut 'em off at the pass." And he slammed the door.

Jermer giggled and Skye allowed herself to smile at Cody's goofiness. But she was still offended by his feeling sorry for her.

"Why did you choose me?" she asked abruptly.

He shrugged. "Because it's Friday. Because it's raining. Because I wanted to treat myself on my birthday by having two nice people to work with."

Jermer sucked in his breath. "Your birthday! Are you having a party?"

Cody smiled. "No party, but with my own eyeballs I saw a cake the size of a football field in Aunt Esta's trunk. What do you want to bet she decorates it with sixteen candles and we have it for lunch, along with a little happy birthday caroling?"

Jermer giggled. "You don't carol on birthdays. That's for Christmas."

But Skye was feeling as if her ears had suddenly shot out antennas. Sixteen! Cody was sixteen! Old enough to drive legally.

"Do you have your driver's license?" she asked.

"Learner's permit," Cody said. "I can drive now with a licensed driver with me, but I'll get my license soon. Now if I only had a car."

Skye's heart beat fast. "I have a car. I mean Reanna and I do." She kept her voice casual. "Reanna left our old station wagon here, and it needs to be driven."

Cody's eyes lit up. "Yeah? Would she mind if I drove it?"

"I'll ask her." She didn't mention that he'd have to drive her off to find Reanna before she could ask. She'd tell him that later. "But it's broken or something. It won't start."

"Well, let's go out and take a look at it right now." Cody headed for the door.

As if she had X-ray eyes, Aunt Esta called, "Cody, are you getting started in there?"

"Absolutely," Cody called back. He grinned at Skye. "Curses. Foiled again. But just wait. We'll go out and check over that car when the time is right."

Skye hoped the time would soon be right. She could hardly contain herself now that she had not only a car but also an almost-licensed driver.

ELEVEN

CODY BEGAN TAKING OLD FAMILY PICTURES
down from the wall as if he'd done this housecleaning thing a million times already. Each spot
where they'd been showed up plain because the
covered places hadn't faded the way the rest of
the old wallpaper had done. Skye thought the
effect was interesting, with the pictures preserv-
ing the paper the way it used to be. It was a little
like the pictures themselves, the way they preserved the memory of how the people used to be.

She and Jermer grabbed the clean rags Aunt
Esta had brought up from the cellar and sat down
on the floor to begin dusting off the pictures. Skye
felt like singing. Things were going to be okay.
After Cody got the car fixed, he could drive her
to Preston where Bill and Reanna would probably have stopped for supplies. She could pick
up some clues there as to which way they went.
Maybe when they bought propane in the hard-

ware store Bill said, "My wife and I, we're heading south." Or north, or west. Bill liked to talk to people. Somebody would know which way they had gone.

Happily Skye polished the glass over the pictures with the vinegar and water solution Aunt Esta had prepared. There were so many of the pictures. She was curious about the two big oval-framed photographs of young men in Army uniforms and asked about them as she dusted and polished.

"One of them is our great-grandfather Rallison," Cody said. "He was the father of your grandpa Orville and my grandma Belva and Aunt Esta and Aunt Vernell. The other picture is of his brother Jack who was killed in World War I back in 1917."

Skye looked at the young face in the picture. "That's sad, Cody."

"Yeah," Cody said. "Grandma says he was engaged to Sweetie Farnsworth's grandmother, but after he died she married somebody else. If he'd lived, Sweetie would have been related to us, and old Jermer here might have been one of our relatives, too."

Skye was surprised. "You mean he isn't? He calls Aunt Esta 'Aunt Esta.' Everybody acts as if he's a relative."

Cody stopped his work long enough to rumple Jermer's hair. "That's because we like him. He's a like-a-lot relative. Isn't that right, Jermer?"

Jermer giggled happily.

"I kind of thought Sweetie must be family, too," Skye said. "She comes to all the family stuff."

Cody lifted down the last picture, then took a clean cloth and began wiping down the wall. "You don't always have to have the same blood to be family," he said.

"Well then, is Jermer . . ." Skye began, glancing at Jermer who was looking up at her. She changed the way she was going to say it. "Jermer, I guess you must be related to Sweetie."

Jermer opened his mouth, then looked at Cody. "Am I?"

"Sure you are, old buddy," Cody said. "Your mother was Sweetie Farnsworth's best friend's daughter. You can't get much more related than that."

"I'm related," Jermer said happily, going back to polishing the glass on one of the photographs.

Things were getting too complicated for Skye to follow. She wished Aunt Esta would go upstairs or something so she and Cody could sneak out to see what was wrong with Reanna's car. In the meantime, she picked up a picture of a young woman in a white dress standing beside a young man in an out-of-style dark suit.

"A wedding picture," Cody said. "That's Aunt Esta and Uncle Harvey when they got married."

He leaned over to pick up another one which he handed to Skye. "Here's Uncle Orville and Aunt Abby on their wedding day."

Orville and Abby. That was Skye's grandpa and grandma. They were standing on kind of a pedestal, which was so the train on Grandma's dress would show up nice, Skye guessed. She carried a bouquet that was a whole lot like the one she'd made for the family history quilt.

Grandpa wore a uniform, a white one with medals on his chest. Did that mean he'd been in the Navy? Skye hadn't even known he'd taken part in a war. For that matter, she hadn't known her great-grandfather and his brother had, either. In fact, she'd never even thought about having a great-grandfather. She'd never thought a whole lot about relatives of any kind before. Reanna always said, "The past is gone. Forget it."

She looked again at the picture of Grandma Abby and Grandpa. This was the way they'd looked before they'd even had Reanna.

"Here, take a look at this." Cody handed her a picture of a baby who peeked out from behind a blanket. A pretty baby, with big blue eyes.

She knew those eyes. "This is Reanna," she said softly. "My mom. When she was a baby."

Jermer got up on his knees so he could lean over her shoulder to look. She could feel his breath on her cheek. "Is that really your mother?"

"That's the way she used to look," Skye said.

Jermer considered that. "Can you remember when she looked that way?"

Skye laughed. "I wasn't born yet, silly."

Jermer's face wrinkled as if he was having a hard time figuring that out. Then he said, "Why did Reanna go away with that guy?"

"They got married, Jermer."

"Why didn't they take you?"

Skye shook her head. "I don't know."

"My dad went away, too," Jermer said. "His name is Jerome."

It was the first time Skye had heard him mention either of his parents. "Why did he go, Jermer?"

He was silent for a moment, then said, "Maybe I was bad." He got to his feet and walked over to look out of the window. "He went to the Snake River."

The vacuum cleaner started roaring upstairs, a perfect sound to cover up attempts to start a car.

"Cody," Skye said, and when he looked over at her, she put her hand to her ear and dangled the car keys she'd kept in her pocket.

He understood.

"Let's go," he said, taking the keys. "Jermer, you stay here and yell for us if you hear Aunt Esta coming."

Jermer shoved out his lower lip in protest. "I want to go with you."

"Hey, we need a lookout," Cody said. "Somebody we can trust. How about it?"

"Well, okay, but promise you won't go anywhere without me."

"Would we leave you behind?" Cody said. "We're the Three Musketeers, Jermer. We won't go anywhere without you. We're just going to take a look at the car."

Jermer still looked suspicious, but he stayed behind as Cody and Skye ran through the drizzly rain.

The station wagon looked worse in the daytime than it had last night, rusty and dented and faded. The tires were good, though. Reanna'd always been particular about the tires.

Cody got into the car and inserted the key. He turned it.

Nothing.

He pulled out a knob. "See if the headlights are on."

Skye went around to the front of the car. "They're not."

"Battery's dead," Cody said.

Skye slumped. Dead. A candidate for Jermer's attentions. Maybe he could just bury the whole dumb car.

"We'll have to jump start it, if we can, and take it into Preston to find out for sure if you need a new battery," Cody said.

So maybe there was hope. "How much is a

new battery?" Skye hardly dared breathe.

"Probably sixty bucks," Cody said.

"Sixty dollars!" He might as well have said a thousand. Skye thought of her little hoard of coins. Nine dollars and seventy-four cents, that's what she had.

But Cody hadn't finished talking. "Tell you what," he said. "If you think Reanna will let me drive the car, I'll donate what Aunt Esta pays me today. Add that to what she pays you, and we'll have a battery fund started."

Skye stared at him through the rain. "I didn't know Aunt Esta was paying us."

"She thinks we should learn how to handle money, and there aren't a whole lot of ways to earn it here in Sheep Creek. She pays us each two dollars an hour whether we're worth it or not." Cody handed the keys back to Skye. "If we're really lucky, the battery might just need a charge. We'll get this sucker started sometime, Skye, and then we'll really roll! Right?"

"Right!" Skye put her face up to the rain, laughing aloud, suddenly as happy as if the raindrops were sunbeams. She wasn't alone any more. Cody was going to help her. Cody, her relative. Her cousin.

TWELVE

THE MONEY FROM AUNT ESTA DIDN'T SOLVE everything, of course.

In the first place, even after six hours of work each Skye and Cody together had earned only twenty-four dollars. That was a long way from sixty dollars, especially if you had no idea how you could earn more. And besides the battery, they'd have to buy gas and probably some food, although Skye figured Grandpa wouldn't mind if she took a couple cans of pork and beans from the shelves in the cellar.

But the biggest problem was still how to find Reanna and Bill.

After Aunt Esta and Aunt Belva and all the cousins finished up the housecleaning and left, Skye hurried upstairs to look again at her tattered map of the western states. Spreading it out on her bed, she studied it, trying to guess where Bill would want to start doing his research on places with interesting names. Would he and Reanna go north to Pocatello? Further west to Declo and Naf? East over the hills to Fish Haven, or maybe on to the Salt River country of Wyoming? Or south into Utah where they'd find Hailstone and Gooseberry and Thistle?

Just reading the names of the towns made Skye yearn to be with Bill and Reanna on those black-and-silver Harleys, right now.

With her finger, she traced highways, remembering the excitement of pulling into a new place full of mystery and possibilities. Of course there never were as many possibilities as Reanna hoped. But they'd stay a while, with Reanna working as a waitress or as a clerk in a Woolworth store or once in a while as a secretary, although Reanna didn't like to type. Then, when they had a little money, they'd move on to another place where Reanna thought she'd find what she was looking for, whatever that was.

Jermer came upstairs while Skye was hunched over the map.

"I wondered where you went," he said. "What are you looking at?"

Skye thought he'd gone home. She wasn't in any mood to entertain him. He buzzed around her like an aggravating fly, breaking into her life, her thoughts. She wanted to flap her hands and say "Shoo," but, remembering how gentle Cody was with Jermer, all she said was, "A map,

Jermer. It's of the western states of the United States." She pointed at a speck near the southern border of Idaho. "Look, here's Sheep Creek where we are. And here's Preston and down here in Utah are Logan and Brigham City."

Would Reanna and Bill have gone that way? Were they even now setting up their tent in the pretty campground south of Brigham City, the one where Skye and Reanna had stopped to rest on their way to Sheep Creek?

Jermer's eyes were enormous as he examined the map. "Is the Snake River on here, too?"

Jermer really had Snake River on his mind.

"Here." Skye let her finger skate along a winding blue line that crossed the entire state of Idaho. "Look, right here it's only about three inches from Sheep Creek."

Jermer glanced at the map, then went over to the window and peered out. "What does it look like, Skye?"

She thought of the big river, slithering its way through its deep, dark canyons. There'd been that time when she and Reanna had stayed in American Falls, a town on the banks of the Snake River, for a couple of months. There was a dam on the Snake at American Falls, and the water backed up behind it to form a lake.

"In some places it's scary. Jermer, did you know that when they dammed the river at American Falls, they moved the whole town to higher ground? The houses, the stores, the school, everything. Then the Snake crawled out of its banks and the water covered up where the town had been."

That was exactly the kind of thing Bill would want to find out for his book. Why hadn't she realized that before when Jermer mentioned the Snake River?

Jermer looked around fearfully. "Did they move the cemetery, too?"

Trust Jermer to think of the cemetery. "Probably."

"All the graves and coffins and everything?"

The kid was spooky. "I don't know, Jermer. Why are you so interested in the Snake River, Jermer?"

His forehead wrinkled. "Maybe I lived there once. Or maybe Sweetie told me about it." He looked out of the window again, as if the Snake might suddenly creep into the yard.

Skye got a red ink pen from her duffel and drew a circle around the town of American Falls on the Snake River. Then she said, "Let's go downstairs and make some cookies, Jermer."

She'd make Glorified Grahams, which was powdered sugar frosting smeared between two graham crackers. Jermer deserved a reward. He'd given her the idea of where she could find Reanna and Bill.

❁   ❁   ❁

The postcard from Reanna came on Saturday. Grandpa handed it to Skye wordlessly when he brought in the mail. It was postmarked Paris, which Skye had seen on her map, a town across the mountains from Sheep Creek, over near Bear Lake.

So they hadn't gone the way she'd guessed they had, that first day. She never would have found them if she'd gone on the milk truck with Mr. Jensen, or even if she'd been able to go look for them in the station wagon.

There wasn't much on the card. All it said was:

Tent leaks. Glad rain is over. Bill is talking with people about Bear Lake. Also asking if Paris was named by people from France. Then we're off again, probably over into Wyoming. Much love. Reanna.

Skye was disappointed. Reanna wasn't even concerned about how she was getting along.

She got her map from upstairs and, as Grandpa watched silently, drew a pencil line from Paris up along Highway 89 in Wyoming, through Smoot and Afton and Thayne. Those little towns were just south of where the Snake River began its flow across the state of Idaho. She was sure that when Bill saw the Snake, he'd want to follow it a while.

On the other hand, he might want to continue

on north through Wyoming to Moose and Jackson Hole and Yellowstone Park.

She'd just have to wait a while, until she got another postcard. By that time the car would probably have its new battery.

At least it would if she could figure out how to earn some more money. Cody had said that jobs were hard to come by in Sheep Creek.

She decided to call him up. She waited until Grandpa went off on his horse again, then took the telephone over by the box of kittens so she could watch them as she talked.

Denise answered. "What do you want to talk to Cody about?" she said when Skye asked for him. "Need to ask him how to spell *cat*?"

Skye heard sounds of a mild scuffle, then Cody said, "Hello?"

There were meows from Denise in the background as Skye asked if Cody had any ideas about getting money.

"Well," he said, "we could rob the bank in Preston, except that we don't have a getaway car until we get your wagon fixed, and we can't get it fixed until we rob the bank."

She laughed just to show him she appreciated his joke. "I mean it, Cody," she said. "I want to get Reanna's car running as soon as we can."

"I want that, too," Cody said. "I've been working for a guy off and on for the past two weeks. I hope he's going to pay me tomorrow. I'll see him at church, then I'll let you know." He paused. "You might ask around and see if any of the ladies need some housework done. Or baby-sitting or something."

He didn't have any more ideas.

After she thanked Cody and hung up, Skye played with the kittens while she thought about what he'd said. She'd never been around babies much, so baby-sitting was out. But she could do housework. What ladies could she ask? The aunts? They lived too far away to walk, and besides their houses were already spotless.

Ignoring the problem for the moment, she took all three of the kittens out of the box and set them on the floor. Twinkie looked at the big world and hissed. Floyd had a take-it-or-leave-it attitude, gazing around without much fear but without a lot of interest, either.

But Oh, tail in the air like a flag, set off immediately to explore the forest of table legs. Dauntless, that's what he was. That was a word Skye had always liked in the poems Reanna had read to her around the campfire with the Fanged Haunts watching from the dark woods behind them. Dauntless, like in "So faithful in love, and so dauntless in war, There never was knight like the young Lochinvar," which was from a poem by Sir Walter Scott.

She'd bet all of her battery fund that Lee Esther

and Know-it-all Denise had never heard of Sir Walter Scott.

Forget them.

Dauntless, that's what she had to be. She'd go right now and ask Sweetie Farnsworth if she needed any work done.

Sweetie was sympathetic but not very helpful. She was playing her old pump organ and singing with Jermer when Skye got there, but she twirled around on the stool and listened while Skye asked about work.

"Take a look, Skye," she said. "I don't live fancy. There's not a whole lot to do here."

Skye looked around the little cabin with rag rugs on the floor, and the big round oak table and the old Monarch wood range with the two-person rocking chair sitting in front of it. Although everything was clean and neat, Sweetie didn't worry about polishing her few pieces of furniture to a high gloss the way the aunts did, and she didn't seem to notice a little dust.

"How about outside?" Skye asked. Sweetie had a huge vegetable garden. Skye could pull weeds or pick beans or dig potatoes.

Sweetie smiled. "I don't have money to pay you even if there was work to do."

She didn't seem embarrassed about saying she had no money, the way some people would be. Reanna was like that, too.

The difference was Reanna had her freedom, and Sweetie didn't. Sweetie had Jermer and this cabin and the garden to tie her down.

But the cabin was cozy and friendly, like Sweetie. It smelled like sunlight and the mint plants outside and the soup Sweetie was simmering on the old wood stove.

"Have you lived here all your life?" Skye asked.

Sweetie seemed surprised at the change of subject, but she said, "No. I've been to just about all the places there are. I used to be a flight attendant for an international airline."

"On airplanes?" Skye caught her breath. Airplanes were the most free of all things, soaring in the air the way they did, heading toward every place in the whole world. "Why did you come back here?"

Sweetie shrugged. "I don't know. I just always knew I'd come back. After I'd been flying for a long time, my grandmother died and left me this old place where she'd been a bride. So I put away my wings and came home."

"Was she the one who was going to marry my great-grandfather's brother who died in a war?" Skye asked.

"Why, yes," Sweetie said. "How did you know?"

"Cody told me."

"Cody likes the old stories, too. There's nothing

114

more fascinating than what went on with your own people before you were born. It kind of lets you know who you are when you know what they were."

"Sweetie." Jermer pulled at Sweetie's sleeve. "Show Skye where the cougar scratched on the house."

"Do you think she'd like to see that?" Sweetie asked.

"You bet," Jermer said enthusiastically.

Skye was full of questions about Sweetie's curious way of living. But she went along when Sweetie slid off the organ stool and motioned for Skye and Jermer to follow her across the kitchen and through a narrow little room filled with shelves to the back door.

"My grandmother used to tell how the big long yellow blowsnakes would crawl into the pantry here back in the old days," Sweetie said.

Skye glanced nervously under the shelves that held bottles of fruit and vegetables and pickles, probably stuff Sweetie had canned herself. She wasn't fond of snakes. "Your grandma was a brave person," she said, "to be able to kill snakes."

"Oh, she didn't kill them," Sweetie said. "Granny never was one for killing, especially snakes that did her a favor by keeping the gopher population down." She picked up a forked stick that stood by the door. "She used this to pick them up and put them back outside."

As Sweetie led the way out of the door and along the back of the house, Skye imagined the young woman who had come to this cabin as a new wife, this girl who should have been Skye's own great-grandfather's brother's bride, except that he died in a war. Suddenly she seemed like a real person rather than just somebody who was dead. She probably looked something like Sweetie and very likely she played the wheezy organ the way Sweetie did now. Probably baked bread in that old stove in the warm, cozy kitchen that made a person feel as if she'd like to sit down there and stay forever.

"Right here," Sweetie was saying. "Here are the scratches the cougar made." She pointed at several deep claw marks in one of the old gray logs.

"It wanted to get inside and eat the people," Jermer said ominously. "But the cabin was too strong." He patted the thick logs as if to thank them.

Sweetie smiled. "It was just a poor hungry wild thing, looking for a meal. Gran said that after it scratched on the house, it went out to the stable and prowled around there, making the horses scream. But everything was closed up tight, and finally it just went away, still hungry."

Skye shivered a little as she imagined how it must have been to be inside the house while the cougar scratched on the outside. It would be like sitting around a campfire knowing the Fanged Haunts were out there in the darkness.

Looking at the scratches, she had the same feeling as she'd had back in Grandpa's parlor, that the past was preserved here, showing what had once been.

As if thinking about Grandpa brought him into being, Skye saw him suddenly appear around the corner of Sweetie's house. He was riding his old gray horse and he looked anxious.

"Well, here's where you are, Sis," he said. "I got right worried when I got home and you weren't there. Thought you might of run off after your ma, the way you were looking at that map so serious like."

Did he suspect that's exactly what Skye had in mind? She couldn't tell. "I just came over to talk with Sweetie, Grandpa," she said. "I forgot to leave a note."

"It's all right," Grandpa said. "It's just that you seemed kind of down after that postcard came."

Skye was surprised that he'd noticed. "We can go on home now," she said. "I was just about to leave anyway."

"Well, before you do, come on in and have some of my soup," Sweetie said. "There's a whole lot more than Jermer and I can eat."

So Grandpa tied his horse to a poplar tree, and they went in and sat around the big oak table in the kitchen. Skye wasn't a penny closer to having the money to get Reanna's car fixed, but as she spooned up her soup, she thought of how safe the little cabin seemed. Safe from cougars and Fanged Haunts and people who tried to claw at a person. But thinking those things only made her uneasy because it wasn't safety she was after. It was freedom, and she wasn't going to have that until the old station wagon was fixed and she was on her way.

THIRTEEN

THE NEXT DAY WAS SUNDAY AND AUNT ESTA called early to say she was coming by to pick up Skye for church.

Skye didn't mind going to church. Sometimes when she and Reanna were traveling and saw a church, they'd stop and go in to sing the hymns and listen to the sermon. Besides, Cody would be there, and he was going to find out if the guy who owed him money could pay him.

Skye thought about riding in Aunt Esta's car with Lee Esther and very likely Denise, too, since Aunt Esta was still determined to get the three of them together. "You don't need to come after me," she said. "I'll ride with Grandpa. He's out in the barn right now, but he'll be in soon. He'll go if I ask him."

Aunt Esta snorted. "Well, go ahead and ask him, but don't be surprised if he suddenly has a stray cow he has to look for. Then again, maybe

119

you can produce a miracle. Let me know if you need a ride." She hung up.

"He'll go," Skye said to the kittens who were hanging by their front paws to the edge of their box, almost able to jump out by themselves.

But she found that miracles weren't that easy to produce.

"I ain't a-goin', Sis," Grandpa said when he came back to the house and she asked him to go with her to church. "Used to go regular when your Grandma Abby was alive. Don't seem to get much out of it anymore."

"I promised Aunt Esta you'd come," Skye said.

"Best never to plan out another body's life," Grandpa said. "Doesn't always work out." He headed toward the bathroom to clean up. "Tell you what. I'll drive you over to Sweetie's and let her drive the truck with you and Jermer. Her old car's been all ailed-up lately."

There seemed to be a lot of that going around, Skye thought, looking out of the window at Reanna's dead car.

While Grandpa scrubbed up, she got dressed in her too long, blue-flowered skirt, the only one she had. With it she wore a plain white shirt and her shabby old brown sandals. She thought about those little white pumps that Denise and Lee Esther had worn to the wedding.

But who cared?

She said good-bye to the kittens, pushing them

back down into the box and petting their soft little bodies. They purred and mewed and stretched up toward her.

"I love you little guys," she whispered, then ran outside to get into Grandpa's truck.

When she and Grandpa got to Sweetie's house, they saw that Sweetie and Jermer were dressed in their Sunday best. Sweetie wore the bright, flowing dress she'd worn to the wedding and Jermer was stuffed into his tight blue suit again.

"See you're all gussied up already," Grandpa said as he got out of the truck. "Want to take a chance on driving this old wreck?"

"Glad to," Sweetie said. "My clunker is totally gone." She flicked a thumb at the gray Dodge that sagged down into the mint plants over by the wooden gate that led to the spring. "The rear axle gave up this morning. No sense trying to fix it up anymore since everything else is worn out. Jermer and I thought we'd just start walking and somebody would pick us up, so we're glad for the wheels."

Grandpa rubbed his chin as he gazed at Sweetie's old car. "If those classes of yours work out for this next week, you can borrow the truck here anytime."

"That's neighborly of you, Orville," Sweetie said. "I might have to do that. Otherwise I'd have to ride one of Jermer's stick horses."

Jermer giggled as he climbed up to sit beside

Skye. Sweetie got into the driver's seat while Grandpa hoisted himself into the back of the truck.

"What kind of classes do you teach?" Skye asked after they dropped Grandpa off at his house and started down the highway. "Quilting," Sweetie said. "Crocheting. Canning fruits and vegetables. Making bread. Smoking meat. All the old home arts that my grandmother taught me. Lots of women are interested in that kind of thing now. Seems like they've got tired of all the instant this and just-add-water that. They want to learn the old ways again."

That seemed exactly the kind of thing that Sweetie should be doing. Skye had never known anybody before who was so much a part of a place the way Sweetie was.

That was probably why she didn't have a telephone or TV.

Skye looked out at the tall sunflowers that lined the highway. Reanna had always said that the past was dead and should be forgotten. But here in Sheep Creek it seemed to be all mixed up with the present and even the future, and Skye was beginning to feel that this was the way it should be.

It was time to leave, for sure, which meant it was time to find homes for the kittens. Maybe someone at church would want them.

✿   ✿   ✿

When they got to the pretty church on the hill, Skye looked around for Cody but didn't see him. Had he forgotten that he was going to see that guy at church and ask about his money? Had he forgotten how anxious Skye was to know if they'd be getting the battery soon?

"We go to classes first," Sweetie said, snagging a couple of passing girls and sending Skye off with them to a room downstairs. The kids in the class were all Skye's own age, so Cody wasn't there since he was older. But the red-haired boy who'd been at Reanna's wedding was part of the class, and he blushed every time he looked at Skye, the way he'd done that day. Denise and Lee Esther were there, too, and they started right off whispering together. About me, probably, Skye thought.

The teacher was nice and welcomed Skye. He was the husband of one of Aunt Belva's daughters, but Skye couldn't remember which one. His name was Ed, but the kids in the class called him Brother Turner.

Somebody wanted to know where Skye was from, and Brother Turner asked if she'd like to tell them.

Skye stood up. "Well, I travel around a lot so I'm not from anywhere. But I would like to say something." She cleared her throat. There were about ten people there besides Denise and Lee Esther, and it made her nervous to have all those eyes looking at her. "I won't be here long, and I need to find homes for some kittens that are at my grandpa's house. Would anybody like a kitten? They're awfully cute, and they're free."

Everybody laughed, and for the moment Skye thought the whole bunch of them were as mean as Denise and Lee Esther. She wished she hadn't opened her mouth. But Brother Turner smiled and said, "They're laughing because around here people are always trying to get rid of kittens. Somebody had some to offer just last week."

So Jermer had been right about nobody wanting the cats. Who else was there to ask?

Reanna and Bill would just have to agree to let Skye take them along. If she could convince them to leave the motorcycles at Grandpa's and travel in the station wagon, they could manage.

She worried about that all through the class discussion, but when everybody went upstairs for the church service the worry changed to anticipation because Cody was there. She'd find out soon if he'd got the money. She'd have to wait until after the service though, because the organ was playing soft music so people would quiet down, and Cody was all the way across the chapel, sitting with friends. Sitting with a *girl*, that's what he was doing. A girl his age with long blonde hair and a blue dress that looked as if she'd snatched it right off Alice in Wonderland.

So what? Skye told herself there was no way

she could be jealous. Cody was her *cousin*, for gosh sake. But the thing was, she wanted him to be interested in getting the car going, not in a girl.

Probably he wanted to have a car so he could take the girl to the movies in Preston. Probably he didn't even care about Skye and *her* problem.

He was going to get quite a surprise when Reanna and Bill decided they needed the station wagon for the kittens, and he was without wheels again.

Despite her thoughts, Skye enjoyed the service, especially the hymn singing. At the start of the meeting, they sang "How Great Thou Art," which Skye was familiar with, and at the end the hymn was one titled "Come, Come Ye Saints," which she didn't know. She liked the way each verse ended with "All is well! All is well!" She hoped it was a good omen.

After the meeting was over, Aunt Esta of course had to catch up with Skye and mention that she didn't see Grandpa present.

It seemed to kind of please her that Skye hadn't been able to get him to come.

"Maybe he'll come next week," Aunt Esta said, "when we're going to have a family dinner afterward down to Vernell's in Preston."

"Maybe," Skye said, twisting her neck around to look for Cody.

Neither he nor that Alice-in-Wonderland girl

were in the chapel, so she went out on the lawn
to look. The red-haired boy was there, blushing
up a storm when Skye glanced his way. Denise
and Lee Esther were there, too. They were standing with some other girls, and all of a sudden they
started singing, "Old MacDonald had a farm, ee-
i-ee-i-oh."

Skye looked around for Cody. Had he gone
on home without even thinking about her?

Behind her, she heard Denise and the other
girls singing, "On that farm he had some cats,
ee-i-ee-i-oh. With a *meow-meow* here, and a *meow-
meow* there . . ."

She turned. They were walking toward her,
some of them putting their hands up like claws
as they came.

It was just one more thing than she could take
right at that moment.

"Scat!" she yelled. "Go eat rats or whatever it
is you creeps live on. *Leave me alone!*"

People stopped their talking to look at her in
puzzlement.

Well, she'd just ruined any chance she had of
making friends in Sheep Creek. She'd be known
all around town as crazy Reanna Rallison's crazy
daughter. So what? She wouldn't be there to
hear.

That "all is well" song was sure a bunch of
hype.

Most of the girls looked startled when Skye

yelled at them, but Denise smiled, that nasty put-down smile that she'd used so often on Skye. Skye wondered if she dared spring at her and maybe claw her eyes right out. That would give people a story to tell and retell like the one about Sweetie's grandmother and the snakes.

She didn't have a chance to do anything to Denise because Sweetie came walking over as if that was what she had in mind anyway, and scooped Skye along with her. "Come on, Skye. We'd better get your granddad's truck back home," she said.

Denise tossed her head. "We were just singing, that's all, Sweetie. I don't know why Skye gets so upset about a little singing."

Sweetie kept right on walking, with her arm around Skye. Jermer scuttled along behind them.

Skye wondered when she'd had a worse day. After Sweetie started up the old truck, she said, "Why does Denise hate me, Sweetie?"

"Well," Sweetie said as she turned toward home along the sunflower-lined road, "Denise has been queen of the roost around here ever since she was old enough to flutter her eyelashes. But you're as pretty as she is and a sight more interesting because you've been all over and seen a lot of stuff that she hasn't, and besides, you're smarter. She's afraid you'll pass her up in school and that people will like you better than they do her."

Skye felt weak. What was Sweetie saying?

"Don't let her get to you. You'll get to be friends after you've been around a while." Sweetie reached over and patted Skye's hand.

She was as bad as Aunt Esta, thinking Skye and Denise and Lee Esther could be friends just because they were the same age.

"I've got good news," Sweetie said. "Those classes I was hoping to teach this week are all set up. I hope your grandpa meant what he said about me borrowing the truck because I have to go to Wyoming until next Saturday."

Jermer bounced on the seat beside Skye. "Can I stay with Skye while you're gone to Wyoming? Can I, Skye?"

"Sure, Jermer." She'd do anything for Sweetie right at that moment, even take care of Jermer. Sweetie, who thought she was pretty, and interesting, too. "Where do you usually stay?"

"Most of the time with Aunt Esta," Jermer said. "But she's mad at me right now because I buried her stuffed parrot last time I was there."

"You can stay with me, Jermer."

It would be something to do while she figured out how to get the battery.

The week went by slowly. Cody called on Monday to say the guy who owed him money hadn't been able to pay him yet and that he was working for another man all that week, driving a hay baler.

He said he'd call when he got paid.

Skye said she hoped Miss Alice in Wonderland wasn't planning on a movie that week, which made Cody laugh and say Miss Alice lived in Preston and could see a movie any old time she wanted to.

So what Cody wanted the car for was to go to Preston every time he had a chance. Well, let him think that's the way it would be.

Jermer wasn't too much trouble, although Skye got mighty tired of playing Monopoly and Go Fish all week long. He slept in the room next to hers, and at least he didn't have nightmares or snore. He did hold a couple of funerals, but he didn't object when she said she didn't want to attend.

Since there were three of them for the noon meal each day, Skye tried several of Reanna's special dishes during the week. Jermer loved everything she fixed, especially the Chili Riot, which was just a can of chili and a can of tamales mixed together, and the Spaghetti Special, which was a can of spaghetti served with a lighted candle set in the middle of the table. Grandpa didn't seem too thrilled with some of the meals, but he ate them, although Skye saw him sneaking a bowl of Shredded Wheat afterward on a couple of days.

Skye and Grandpa had only one disagreement all week, and that was about whether Skye needed to get registered for school. Skye said she wasn't going to go to school there, and Grandpa said it was the law and she had to. She said she was leaving, and he said not to count on it. He said Aunt Esta would take her to Preston to register since she'd said she wanted to make sure Skye and Denise and Lee Esther all got into the same class. Skye said she'd rather have pencil leads shoved under her fingernails than be in a classroom with Denise, which made Grandpa smile. Apparently he understood about Denise.

"Well then, ask Sweetie to take you to the school," he said, and that's how they left it.

Saturday morning Sweetie came home. Skye took Jermer up to her house while she was unloading the truck.

To her surprise, she handed Skye a twenty-dollar bill.

"They paid me quite well," she said, "and I know you were looking to earn some money."

"Wow." Skye made some calculations in her head. "Wow, I've almost got enough now."

"Going to buy a new dress?" Sweetie asked.

"I'm going to buy a new battery for Reanna's car," Skye told her. "It needs to be driven, and Cody wants to drive it, so he's putting in some money, too."

She didn't say any more of her plans. Sweetie wouldn't approve of her taking off after Reanna any more than Grandpa would.

"A battery," Sweetie said. "Why didn't you say

so before? That's about the only thing that's any good in that old wreck of mine. Cody can come and get it any time and put it in Reanna's car."

Skye could hardly breathe. She had a battery. She could be on her way to look for Reanna and Bill as early as tomorrow!

That hymn had been right after all. All is well, she thought.

She could hardly wait to tell Cody.

FOURTEEN

JERMER FOLLOWED SKYE HOME, TRAILING BE-
hind her like a lost puppy.

"Skye," he called, "wait for me. Do you want
to play No Bears Out Tonight? Or Gray Wolf,
maybe?"

"No," Skye yelled over her shoulder. "You'd
better go home."

But he came on, stumbling over the rocks,
dragging that dumb blue backpack with him.

He came in handy, though, when they got to
Grandpa's house and Skye didn't want to take a
chance on talking to Denise again. She had
Jermer call and ask for Cody.

"Denise answered," he said when he hung up.

"So what did she say?"

Jermer put his hands on his hips. "She said,
'He's not here. Why do you want to talk to him
anyway, you little twerp?'" He dropped his
hands. "Denise doesn't like me."

Skye felt a flash of anger. It was bad enough for Denise to snarl at *her*, but why did she have to chew up a baby like Jermer?

"Denise doesn't like anybody," she said. "Let's play with the kittens."

Two of the kittens had discovered how to get out of their box. Probably Oh had figured it out first, then showed Twinkie. The two of them were exploring the kitchen. Placid Floyd seemed content to stay at home in the box.

What kind of travelers would Oh and Twinkie be if they wouldn't stay in their box? Would they be scared and yowl the way Babe had done?

"Let's take them outside," Skye said. "They need to get used to the world."

Babe was nervous about having her babies running loose outside, and for a few minutes she tried to herd them, swatting them lightly when they wandered too far from her. But soon she relaxed, crouching on the porch where she had a good view of all of them. Skye and Jermer sat on the steps beside her.

"Why do you want to start Reanna's car?" Jermer asked.

Skye watched Floyd follow the progress of a bug who struggled through the blades of grass. "So Cody can drive it."

"Where to, Skye? Are you going to have him drive it to the Snake River?"

How did he know? Looking at him, Skye decided he was just guessing. He had the Snake River on his mind.

"Maybe, Jermer. Let's go call again and see if Cody's home yet."

"Take me with you, Skye."

She stood up. "You can come. But I won't make you call this time."

"I mean take me with you to the Snake River."

"I can't do that. Why do you want to go, anyway? Don't you like it at Sweetie's?"

He stood up, too. "I love it at Sweetie's," he said. "But I don't want you to go away without me."

"Jermer, I have to look for somebody. I have to find my mother. That's why I have to go."

"I have to look for somebody, too."

"Who, Jermer? Your mother?"

He shook his head. "I know where my mother is." He scuffed the toe of his shoe against the porch step. "Way down deep," he said softly, then looked up. "I'll call Cody again if you want me to, Skye."

"I'll do it, Jermer." It always made Skye feel bad to remember Jermer's mother was dead. "I'll call, and if Cody can come over now, you can watch us change the battery in Reanna's car."

Cody's mother answered this time. "He's working for Mr. Rasmussen, Skye," she said. "He'll be there until after dark. They have to finish baling the hay tonight, what with tomorrow being

134

Sunday and all, and maybe a storm coming up."

Skye thanked her and hung up. "How far away is Mr. Rasmussen's field?" she asked Jermer. She felt anxious about letting Cody know they had a battery, as if it might somehow disappear if they didn't get it right away.

"It's just behind Cougar Hill," Jermer said. "We can walk up and follow the water ditch around and find him."

"Let's go." Skye was glad now that Jermer had come. She was good enough at finding places that were on maps, but all the valleys and hills of Sheep Creek confused her and she wasn't sure she could find Mr. Rasmussen's field by herself.

Outside, they saw that Grandpa had returned, riding that old gray horse of his. Tarzan was there, too, bounding toward the house, his eyes on . . .

The kittens! Oh, no! Skye felt as if her heart had stopped. She'd forgotten about the kittens being out on the lawn, and now Tarzan was there.

Babe saw him and advanced, back arched, ears laid back, tail puffed to three times its normal size.

Floyd and Twinkie were behind Babe, over near the house, tumbling over one another in their play. But where was Oh?

Tarzan spotted him at the same time Skye did, on the edge of the lawn by Reanna's old car, watching a butterfly. Tarzan's ears flipped forward. He rushed toward the kitten.

At Skye's side, Jermer moaned.

"Don't panic, Sis," Grandpa called from his seat on the horse. "Don't startle either one of them."

Tarzan was almost on top of Oh when the kitten saw him. Suddenly Oh was a small version of his mother, standing on his claws, ballooning to spiky ferocity.

Tarzan stopped. He stared. Slowly he inched his big muzzle forward. One snap, that's all it would take. He could swallow Oh whole, if he wanted to.

But all he did was sniff at the kitten, then turn and amble back toward Grandpa, tail swishing, tongue flopping casually out of his mouth as if he didn't care a fig about cats.

Skye was weak with relief. She'd had such nightmares about Tarzan harming the kittens. She'd been afraid he was a cat killer. "Good Tarzan," she called.

Jermer rushed out to pick Oh up and hug him to his chest.

"Didn't really think old Tarzan would hurt anything, but you can't ever be sure," Grandpa said, getting down from his horse. "You off to somewhere, Sis?"

Skye had all but forgotten the battery in her fright over the kittens. "Jermer and I were going to go talk to Cody." She walked over to pat Tarzan as she spoke. "Grandpa, I thought it'd be a good idea to keep up Reanna's car. Cody would like to drive it a little, just to keep it going." She continued to pat Tarzan as she told Grandpa about the dead battery and about Sweetie having a good one.

Grandpa nodded as she spoke. "Sounds all right to me. You got good sense there, Sis."

Skye felt a little flattered and a whole lot guilty about not telling him what else she had in mind. "Grandpa," she said, "do you think it's all right to leave the kittens out here? They like their freedom, and Tarzan's not going to bother them."

"Tarzan's not the only thing that might hurt them," Grandpa said. "But you go along. I'll put them back in their box."

Skye was pleased to see how gently he picked up the kittens in his big hands.

Jermer showed Skye a faint footpath leading up the hill and along the banks of the irrigation ditch that ran around the mountain. From up there, the fields were like Grandma Abby's family history quilt, each patchwork piece with someone's house or the church or the old yellow schoolhouse on it.

Sheep Creek wound through the pieces like a miniature Snake River, twisting and turning and flowing out of the valley to wherever it went.

Did the highway that led to Preston follow the

route of Sheep Creek? Or did it turn off into one of the other valleys Skye could see?

Cody would know.

As they walked along the ditchbank, Jermer sang a song about a bear who went over a mountain to see what he could see, but when he got there all he saw was the other side of the mountain.

"I learned that from Sweetie," he said. "She sings it whenever we walk over one of these hills."

It was a nice song, but Skye figured Sweetie must have forgotten all the things that were on the other side of the mountain or she'd still be out there seeing them.

As Skye and Jermer came around a jutting of the hill, they could see Cody down in a field driving the big, noisy hay baler. When they got down to him, they found he wasn't alone. The red-haired guy who blushed whenever he was around Skye was there beside him in the cab of the hay baler, and he started right in to turning red the minute he saw her.

"Hi, Skye," Cody said, stopping the motor of the baler. He nodded toward the red-haired boy. "You know my copilot Brad?"

"Sort of," Skye said. "I didn't know his name. Hi, Brad."

Brad fired up a little more and muttered something that Skye figured was some kind of greeting.

"Cody," she said. "We've got a battery."

Cody got down from the machine. "You mean one just fell out of the blue?"

"Almost." Skye was going to tell him about it, but Brad started up the baler and drove off along the next swath of alfalfa, making so much noise that it was useless to try to talk.

When he could be heard, Cody flipped a thumb in the direction of the baler. "Brad, there, he's showing off. For you, Skye."

"Sure," Skye said.

Cody grinned. "Believe me. I know what it's like to be a young guy when a pretty girl comes along. You want to show her how manly you are."

He probably had a lot of experience in that department, showing off for that Alice-in-Wonderland girl, Skye thought. But she felt her cheeks color up a little, the way Brad's did. Nobody except Sweetie had ever called her a pretty girl before.

Brad turned halfway down the row and came back, maneuvering the huge machine expertly. Right in front of them he whipped it around and went the other way again.

Showing off.

For her!

Cody watched him. "Look at him go. His dad figures he's too young to handle it all alone, which is why I'm here. But he's a real tiger."

Brad didn't look like much of a tiger. He was

skinny and just barely as tall as Skye, and then there was all that blushing. If he'd been more like Cody, tall and a little older, it might have been kind of exciting to have Brad interested in her. But mostly what Skye felt was embarrassed about him putting on a show for her benefit.

On the other hand, it wasn't a totally unpleasant feeling.

"So tell me about that battery," Cody said.

Skye didn't know where to put her eyes while she told about Sweetie's battery. She didn't want to appear to be watching Brad, but she didn't want to look right at Cody's grinning face, either.

"Whoopee," Cody said when she finished telling about Sweetie's old car and how it didn't need its parts anymore. He whapped his hand against his thigh, raising a cloud of dust. "Let me call off Brad and we'll go get that battery and put it in Reanna's car. We may have that sucker running before the moon comes up."

The fact was, the moon was just peeking over Cougar Hill by the time Reanna's car coughed and started up, after its battery transplant.

Brad had come along to help install it. He'd handed tools to Cody the way nurses handed things to doctors in the shows on TV. He hadn't said a word to Skye, but now and then she caught him looking at her.

Cody was jubilant when the car started, but no less than Skye.

Even Jermer was excited. "Are we going to leave tonight, Skye?" he asked.

"Leave?" Cody looked puzzled.

"I want you to take me someplace," Skye said. "Remember, I told you about it."

"Well, we won't be going anywhere tonight," Cody said. "I don't have my driver's license yet, remember? I can't get into Preston until Monday or maybe Tuesday to get it."

Monday or Tuesday. How long would it take Bill and Reanna to get over to American Falls from Wyoming, if that's the way they went? How long would they stay?

Skye didn't want to take the chance of missing them. Now that the car was running, she'd just drive it herself, the way she'd planned to do in the first place.

In fact, she'd leave that very night.

FIFTEEN

Skye really meant to leave that night.

But just how should she go? On the map it looked so simple to get from Sheep Creek to American Falls, on the Snake River, especially once she got to the interstate highway, which showed as a wide red line.

But it was that narrow black line on the map connecting Sheep Creek to Preston that stopped her. There were less than fifteen miles of twisting road that somehow wound itself down out of the mountains and onto the flatlands of a broad valley. She thought of all those little valleys she'd seen from the hillside with Jermer, each one with a road running through it. Which road led to Preston? The country roads weren't marked well the way the interstates were, and in the dark she might take the wrong one. She couldn't ask for directions. Who would believe she was old

142

enough to be driving? They'd send her back to Grandpa.

And then there was the almost-empty gas tank. What was she going to do about that? The gas stations might be closed.

Exhausted from thinking, she finally slept.

She awoke in the morning to hear Grandpa say, "Nosirree, I ain't a-goin'," in his talking-to-Aunt-Esta voice. "Duty or no duty, I ain't a-goin'." He was silent for a while, then said, "Well, I'll ask her."

Skye heard him come to the bottom of the stairs.

"Sis," he bellowed. "Phone."

Skye hurried downstairs. It was Aunt Esta, all right.

"Get dressed," she commanded when Skye picked up the telephone. "I'm going to pick up you and Sweetie and Jermer for church today because we're all going to Aunt Vernell's for a family reunion dinner afterward. Although," she added, "*some* of the family won't be there."

She was talking about Grandpa, of course. Skye thought of saying, "Nosirree, I ain't a-goin'," the way he'd done. Church and dinner would take up the biggest part of the day. She needed to get started on her trip to American Falls.

But maybe there'd be fewer cars later — and less possibility of the highway patrol being out.

Besides she wasn't at all sure that Aunt Esta would grant her the freedom of choice.

Without waiting for her to say anything at all, Aunt Esta said, "Now hurry, Skye," and hung up.

It wasn't until Skye was rounding up the kittens, all of whom had discovered how to get out of their box, that she remembered Aunt Vernell lived in Preston. Preston, where the gas stations were.

Things were falling into place, the way pieces of a jigsaw puzzle did once you determined what the total picture was going to be.

Skye made Cheese Monsters for breakfast as kind of a farewell gift to Grandpa, although he didn't know she'd be leaving, of course. They didn't work out too well because the Bisquick biscuits crumbled and she scorched the fried eggs, but he ate all of his and said, "Thanks, Sis. Right tasty."

Cody was at church, sitting again with Alice in Wonderland. This time she had on a pink dress. Maybe she lived in Preston as Cody said, but she sure must spend a lot of time on the road coming to Sheep Creek.

Brad was there, too. He managed to give Skye a bashful grin after which he practically set the whole place afire with those bright red blushes he was so good at.

Denise and Lee Esther couldn't help but notice

what was going on. Denise mouthed, "Brad loves Skye," and Skye figured she and everybody else would be hearing a whole lot about it later.

After church, it wasn't hard to convince Cody to drive Reanna's car to Preston. In fact, Skye merely mentioned she'd like to get the gas tank filled and he all but went into orbit.

"I'll drive it down to Aunt Vernell's," he said. "Sweetie and Jermer can ride with us so I'll have a licensed driver with me."

He was careful about things like that. Skye wondered how he'd take to the news that she was setting off all by herself, unlicensed as a skunk.

Would he still like her?

Did she care if he liked her? As soon as Skye got away from there, he could spend his entire total twenty-four hours a day with Miss Alice if he wanted to.

Aunt Esta grumbled about taking everybody back to Grandpa's place to get the car. "Are you sure it's running all right?" she asked. "Are you sure it won't collapse somewhere down by the river where you can spend the rest of the afternoon fishing or picnicking or something?"

Cody promised they'd get there, and Sweetie told Aunt Esta not to worry about it.

While they were at Grandpa's, Skye had time to run upstairs and grab a notepad and pencil from her stuff. Then as they drove along in the car, with Cody and her in the front seat and

Sweetie and Jermer in back, she sketched each intersection and which way to turn.

Although she tried to do it casually, as if she were just doodling, Sweetie noticed and said, "Planning to go somewhere, Skye?"

"I'm the navigator when Reanna and I are on the road," Skye said. "I always watch how we get places."

Sweetie nodded. "Good habit to get into." She was silent for a few minutes while Cody drove carefully along the winding mountain road. Then she said, "We'd better get you registered in school this week," which Skye didn't see was connected to anything, but then Sweetie went on to say, "You've been to so many places you're sure to win all the honors in geography."

It was a thing Skye'd always liked, geography, but she'd never won any honors. She'd be in a school just long enough for a teacher to know her name, then she and Reanna would move on to another town.

"I'll be leaving before school starts," she said and immediately wished she hadn't for fear Jermer would grab onto it and ask again when they were leaving, the way he'd done the night before with Cody.

But Jermer was asleep beside Sweetie, clutching his blue backpack against his chest, that dumb backpack with the peanut butter and boiled eggs

146

he always carried with him. His head was in Sweetie's lap, and she stroked his hair the way Skye stroked the kittens' fur while they slept. It made Skye think of what Sweetie'd said about all the soft, sweet things that needed to be taken care of.

"Then Reanna's coming back to get you after all," Sweetie said.

Skye didn't like the way that sounded. "Reanna didn't want to leave me in the first place. How would you like to go off and leave your very own baby who's been with you since the day she was born? It wasn't easy for Reanna to go without me."

"For pity sakes, I wasn't criticizing your mother," Sweetie said. "We all do what we have to do."

"She knows I can't stay here. She knows I have to be free." Skye turned around to look at Sweetie as she said it.

Sweetie looked out of the window. "One person's freedom is another person's prison," she said so softly that Skye wasn't even sure that's what she'd said.

She didn't say anymore and neither did Skye.

They filled up the gas tank at a service station before going to Aunt Vernell's. Cody insisted on paying for it since he said he'd be the one driving the car after he got his license. Skye felt bad about letting him think that. Maybe she could send him the money later.

Aunt Vernell's house was two stories high and sprawled across a big lot with trees and flowers all around it, but it was still too small to hold all the people who were there. There were people out on the lawn and people in the living room and hallways and kitchen. There were little kids playing out under the trees and bigger kids watching TV in the family room.

There were several older people who Cody said were cousins of the aunts and grandpa. All of them made a point of welcoming her, although they'd ask, "Now who is it you are?"

"I'm Skye, Reanna's daughter," she'd tell them, and they'd nod and say, "Oh, yes, Reanna. That's Orville's girl who ran off with that McCabe boy. He was Alf McCabe's son. Alf, he was the one who took the high school basketball team to the state championship way back in — what year was that? Tall, he was. Captain of the team."

"Don't mind them," Cody whispered to Skye. "They won't remember your name the next time they see you, but they have the whole history of everybody in the county stored in their heads. They can tell you everything that's happened in the last seventy-five years."

What Skye wanted to hear more about was "that McCabe boy." Scott McCabe, her father.

And Alf — he would be her grandfather. The captain of the basketball team that had taken the state championship so many years ago.

Reanna'd never wanted to talk about Skye's father nor his family, so just about all Skye knew about them was what Grandpa had told her about her dad. She didn't even know where he was.

Did he know where *she* was?

She wondered if he cared.

She didn't get a chance to ask anybody about her father during the dinner, which was mountains of mashed potatoes, gallons of gravy, huge haunches of beef, and tubs of string beans, all cooked to perfection despite the large quantities. Very likely the potatoes and beans and the crisp celery stalks and carrot strips that stood at attention in tall glasses on each table all came from Aunt Vernell's garden, which stretched out almost a block long behind the house, with apple and apricot and cherry trees at the far end.

All of the relatives were catching up on everybody else's activities while they ate, and Skye didn't want to break in to ask about her father. Maybe she and Reanna would come back next year or sometime, and Skye could ask then.

But some of the relatives looked very old. Would they still be around then?

After dinner everybody sat around and talked some more. Aunt Vernell's house was a lot like Grandpa's, only bigger, with some of the same family pictures hanging on the walls. It was spotlessly clean, but not so much so that you felt you needed to take your shoes off, the way you did in Aunt Esta's house. There was a stuffed feeling about Aunt Vernell's house because all the bookcases were overflowing with books, and tabletops were covered with jigsaw puzzles or other games, and there were two freezers in the big kitchen filled with frozen casseroles and hunks of meat and pies and cakes.

Aunt Vernell herself was pillow-shaped like Aunt Belva and Aunt Esta, only plumper. She was nice to hug.

She hugged Skye tightly when it was time to go and said she looked forward to getting better acquainted. "I've got tons of old pictures you'd like to see." She waved a hand at one of the stuffed bookcases. "Come and spend a day with me sometime."

"Aunt Vernell," Skye said, "do you know where my dad is?"

Aunt Vernell looked as if she was thinking. "Well, mercy, I don't think I do right now. He used to send a card at Christmas and ask if we'd heard anything about you."

Well, a person couldn't expect *everything* to work out all at once.

Disappointment must have showed on Skye's face, because Aunt Vernell went on to say, "Tell you what I'll do. I'll see if I can find the address of some of his kin. They don't live around here anymore."

"Thanks, Aunt Vernell," Skye said.

It hadn't been such a bad day. The best thing about the whole afternoon was that there were so many people Skye hardly saw Denise and Lee Esther at all.

It was after three when Cody drove the station wagon back down Grandpa's lane and nosed it in under the cottonwood trees where it had been living. They'd already dropped Sweetie and Jermer off at home.

"Well, it's not my dream car," Cody said, "but it's wheels and I like it. Now where is it you want me to drive you as soon as I get my license?"

"You don't need to drive my anywhere," Skye said. "I changed my mind."

Cody looked at her curiously. "Okay. Let me know if you change it again." He got out and loped off down the road toward his own house.

Skye thought about offering to drive him home since it was almost three miles to his house. But he'd very likely give her a lecture on breaking the law. Besides, she didn't want *anybody* to know she could drive.

After Cody left, Skye went inside and found the kittens playing around the table legs. Babe lay on her side, placidly watching them. Skye wished she had time to watch for a while, too, but she had to hurry.

Grandpa was stretched out on the living room couch, snoring softly, taking his Sunday afternoon nap. Perfect. She could load up the cats and her stuff and get out of there before he woke up. She'd be able to get to American Falls before it was too dark, now that she knew the way to Preston. It was a cinch to get to the interstate from there.

She got her duffel and jacket and map from upstairs and put them, along with a bottle of water, in the car.

Next she went to get the kittens and Babe.

Babe didn't take to the car any better this time than the last time Skye had tried to put her in. She yowled and hissed and clawed at the windows, and when Skye brought the boxful of kittens and opened the door to put them in, Babe escaped.

Well, she'd find her later. The kittens were too young to be without their mother yet, so she couldn't leave Babe behind.

The kittens weren't much better. When she set the box down in the back of the car, they spilled out and began a major exploration. They crawled over the seats and under the seats and Twinkie got caught between a seat and a door, mewing so loud Skye thought for sure Grandpa'd wake up, especially when Tarzan came over to bark at the noise.

So what was she going to do? How could she

keep her wits while she looked at the sketches she'd made about which way to turn at the intersections? How could she keep calm on the interstate with Babe howling and the kittens crawling around, onto the gas pedal and under the brake and all over?

She'd have to leave them all.

What other way was there?

Reanna would bring her back to pick them up. Grandpa would watch over them for a day or two.

She wished she didn't remember what Grandpa had said about not planning out what another body would do.

Quickly she hauled the box back into the house and wrote a note for Grandpa, explaining why she had to go. The kittens were out of the box before she had it half written, but there wasn't any use putting them back in. When she went out, she left the kitchen door halfway open so Babe could get in to watch them. Oh started to follow her, so she ran quickly across the lawn. Maybe he'd lose sight of her.

Grandpa would be waking up any minute. Back in the car, Skye turned the key, hoping he wouldn't hear the engine noise.

The car didn't want to start.

"Come on, come on," she whispered as she tried it again. "You've been running so well today."

The car started, and she was just figuring out the best way to back it up so she could head toward the highway when she saw Sweetie and Jermer coming down the path from the calf pasture. Sweetie waved her hand, making motions for Skye to wait.

Skye shifted into reverse and stepped on the gas.

Jermer began to run toward her. "Skye," he screamed. "Stop. Stop. STOP!"

Sweetie, too, was yelling and making some kind of frantic gestures.

Skye wasn't going to let them stop her. Not now when freedom was so close.

She looked into the sideview mirror as she backed up and caught a mere glimpse of Oh, dauntless, foolish little Oh, just before the wheel of the car passed over him.

Sweetie was a good person to have around when something hideous happened. She grabbed Skye before she could even look at what she'd done and turned her toward the house.

Grandpa was there on the kitchen steps by then, rubbing his head and looking alarmed at all the screaming.

"Take care of it, Orville," Sweetie said as she pushed Skye past him, into the house.

She kept Skye walking until they got to the living room where she let her collapse on the couch, which was still warm from Grandpa. Sweetie sat beside her, holding her tight, patting her back, crooning softly to her. "There, there, there," Sweetie crooned.

Reanna had never said, "There, there, there."

The old kitchen clock struck four.

Skye couldn't cry. She was too numb. Too icy and rigid. "He followed me out," she whispered, shivering.

Grandpa had said that there were other things out there besides Tarzan that might harm the kittens, but she'd never, never, NEVER thought it might be her.

SIXTEEN

JERMER OFFERED TO CONDUCT A FUNERAL.

He and Grandpa stood there on Grandma Abby's rose-colored carpet, gazing down at Sweetie and Skye. Jermer was sobbing and he kept wiping his running nose with the bottom of his T-shirt. But he seemed determined to say what he had to say.

"We'll invite the aunts and the cousins," he said. "It'll make you feel better, Skye." He reached out to hold her hand.

His voice seemed to come to her through a long, hollow tunnel. The words didn't make sense.

"It'd be good to do that, Sis," Grandpa said.

He and Jermer had come into the house after doing whatever they had to do with what was left of little Oh. Behind them Skye could see the oval pictures of Great-grandfather Rallison and his brother Jack who'd been killed in World War I.

She thought about having all the aunts and cousins come, thought about them looking at her, knowing what she'd done. Denise and Lee Esther would be there, snickering behind their hands, watching to see if she was going to be a baby and bawl all over the place again. Cody would come, and he'd know she'd tried to drive off by herself. Cody, who wouldn't think of breaking the law.

Well, let them come then. Let them see what a total disaster she was. Let them remember her as the girl who ran over her own pet. That's what she deserved, wasn't it?

She opened her mouth to tell Jermer he could plan a funeral, but all that came out was a wail, a long, drawn-out, hoarse bellow that Skye had never heard before coming from herself.

Sweetie pulled her close again. "We'll talk about it later, Jermer," she said. She smoothed Skye's hair. "Go ahead and holler, honey. It'll make you feel better."

Why was everybody telling her what would make her feel better? She was never going to feel better.

But she still couldn't cry. She couldn't even talk. She felt as frozen inside as those chickens and casseroles in Aunt Vernell's freezer. All she could do was moan.

She huddled there on the sofa for a long time while Sweetie held her close. She must have slept then, because the next thing she knew she was stretched out and Jermer was standing over her whispering, "Are you awake, Skye?"

She drew a long, quivery breath. "Yes," she said. At least she could talk now, although her throat hurt and she was hoarse.

Jermer knelt beside the sofa and took one of her hands. "Are you okay?" he whispered.

She nodded.

"I got scared," he whispered, "about the way you looked after . . . after . . ." He let go of her hand and scrubbed at his eyes with his own. "Skye, what songs would you like me to sing at the funeral?"

Skye thought of the way he sang. "Does Sweetie know some funeral songs?" she asked, hoping that wouldn't hurt his feelings.

It didn't. "Lots," he whispered. "That's who I learned them from. She sings nice."

Skye sat up. From the kitchen she heard Sweetie talking on the telephone. "You don't have to whisper, Jermer."

"I know. It's just because I feel so bad." He lifted the bottom of his T-shirt to wipe his nose again.

"Me, too," Skye whispered.

But she still couldn't cry.

Grandpa came back then. He held a box that was covered in blue cloth, all puffed and padded so that it didn't even look like the shoe box that it very likely was.

"Reckon this would make a right nice casket," he said. "Your Grandma Abby made it in one of them doodad craft classes the church ladies have." He handed it to her.

Skye touched its satiny sides. "It's so pretty. Are you sure you want use it for . . . for . . ." Her throat was so tight that she couldn't say the word. "Are you sure you want to bury it? We could use something else."

"Use it," he said, sitting down on a nearby chair. "Unless you want to keep it."

She couldn't keep it. Reanna always said it just weighted you down to hang onto things, especially useless things like a pretty box.

"We'll use it," Skye said. "Thanks, Grandpa."

Sweetie came back from phoning and sat beside Skye again. "I called the family. They'll be coming."

Coming? Coming for what? For a funeral for a kitten?

Skye was going to ask about it, but Jermer whispered, "We'd better pick a place for Oh's grave," and they all got up to go.

The worst part was going through the kitchen where Babe was bathing her two remaining kittens, tonguing them so enthusiastically that they couldn't even stay on their feet. Did she know her other baby was gone? Did she even think about it?

Skye hurried through the room, not even stopping to pet the cats.

Jermer thought the orchard would be a nice place for a cemetery, somewhere under the old apple trees that Skye's great-grandfather had planted. Great-grandfather Rallison, whose picture hung in the living room. He'd planted all those trees.

"Over here's where I buried my dog Sport when I was a boy," Grandpa said, pointing to a tree that bent low with its load of green apples. "Some cats here, too. Esta, she used to like cats before she grew up and got so tarnation particular about her house. Your grandma had me put a couple of her favorite cats here, too."

"How about Reanna?" Skye asked. "Didn't she have pets?"

"Nope," Grandpa said. "Reanna never took to animals. Nor to much of anything else around here," he added as he went off to get a shovel.

It wasn't long until cars started to arrive: Aunt Esta's big car full of grandkids, and the van that belonged to Denise and Cody's parents. Cody was driving it, with his dad beside him and the rest of the family and Brad Rasmussen in the back. Aunt Belva's car came, and even Aunt Vernell's from Preston, all of them full of people.

The aunts brought casseroles and cakes and homemade rolls. Skye wondered for a minute how they'd managed to throw together all that food just since Sweetie called, but then she thought of the stuffed freezer she'd seen at Aunt Vernell's house. The aunts, like Boy Scouts, were always prepared.

The funeral was nice, as long as Skye held on to her numbness. Jermer scurried around, bringing a chair for her to sit on next to the grave, telling people where to stand, finding an old wooden crate for the pretty casket to fit into so dirt wouldn't get on it.

Sweetie sang "Will the Circle Be Unbroken?", which Skye had asked for. Jermer said a few words about the kitten, telling some of the funny things he'd done in his short life, like how he'd hang onto the edge of the box with his claws and how he'd stood up to Tarzan. The people chuckled a little, only not too much since this was a sad occasion, after all. The service ended with Sweetie singing "Rock of Ages," her voice high and clear in the twilight of the old orchard.

Grandpa had to turn on the yardlight so they could see to eat out on the lawn. Skye saw Denise and Lee Esther there on the edge of the darkness, but they weren't meowing at her this time, although Denise was whispering into Lee Esther's ear, as usual.

But at least they couldn't say she was crying.

Brad Rasmussen came up and told Skye how sorry he was about her kitten. "I hope you're in my class when school starts," he said. His freckled face flared as bright as the yardlight, and he ran off to punch Cody on the arm.

Skye couldn't read Cody's face. He must know now that she'd just been using him to get the car fixed. He hadn't said much to her, but he helped Jermer fill up the grave after Sweetie's song.

Through it all, Skye didn't shed a single tear. Not even when each of the aunts hugged her as they left. Not even when Lee Esther came over and threw her arms around Skye and gave a little sob that Skye felt rather than heard. "I'm real sorry about the cat, Skye," she whispered. When Denise glared at her, Lee Esther glared right back.

Denise didn't say anything at all. Skye didn't expect her to.

She didn't shed a single tear, even though this was a good-bye to all the relatives as well as to the kitten. She wouldn't be coming back here. Somebody would take her to find Reanna now that she'd shown what a criminal she was, and she'd never come back again.

With Grandpa's permission, Sweetie took Skye to her house to sleep that night.

Skye didn't object. She wasn't going to sleep anyway. She was going to lie all night long going over that terrible moment in her mind, trying to make it all unhappen. She knew that's what she'd do, so what did it matter where she was?

Sweetie built a little fire in her old wood stove. It felt good even though the evening was warm enough.

"Why don't we sing a while?" Sweetie said, seating herself on the organ stool. "Singing can take your mind off things you don't want to think about."

Jermer wanted to sing, "Oh, the horse went around with his foot off the ground," so Sweetie started pumping the wheezy old organ and Jermer sang all the verses in his raspy voice. There was only the one line, and each verse left off one word so that the final verse was total silence.

Skye managed a little laugh when it was finished, mainly because Jermer thought it was so funny and she wanted to please him.

"Are there some songs you want to sing?" Sweetie asked.

Skye thought about the songs Reanna had sung to her: "Where Have All the Flowers Gone?" and one she said her own mother had sung to her about some children lost in the woods. "Oh, poor little babes, Oh, babes in the woods," it went.

Sad songs.

Did Reanna sing only sad songs?

"No," Skye said. "There aren't any I want to sing."

Sweetie stood up. "Maybe we should just talk instead." She motioned for Skye to sit with her in the two-person rocker on the rag rug in front of the stove.

"I'll make popcorn," Jermer said, lifting a long-handled contraption from a nail behind the stove. He poured popcorn into it, then skated it back and forth on top of the stove until the corn began to pop.

Neither Aunt Esta nor Grandpa, not even Cody, had asked what Skye thought she was doing, driving off in the station wagon the way she'd tried to do. Sweetie didn't ask either, but Skye felt she had to explain.

"I was going to find Reanna," she said. "I can't stay here. I have to be free. Reanna says that's the most important thing."

Sweetie didn't say anything, just rocked back and forth, back and forth, keeping an arm snug around Skye.

"The kittens," Skye said. "I didn't want to leave them. I promised Aunt Esta I'd take care of them and find homes before I left. But I had to go and they didn't like the car. I was going to ask Reanna to bring me back to get them all. But Oh followed me."

Sweetie rocked silently.

"Do you think Reanna would have brought me back to get them?" Skye asked.

"It would be pretty hard to carry a batch of

cats along with you when you're traveling on motorcycles, Skye," Sweetie said.

"We'd go in the station wagon," Skye insisted. "Reanna would do that, wouldn't she, since I want the cats so much?"

"I don't know," Sweetie said softly. "What do you think, honey?"

Skye didn't want to think. She had to believe Reanna would scoop up all the cats and they'd all travel happily ever after. "I love those cats," she said.

Sweetie was silent.

"It doesn't matter to Reanna what anybody else wants." The words burst from Skye as if they had to be said.

"Skye," Sweetie said. "That isn't the whole of Reanna. Think about the good things. She cares about the family and all. She came back here for her wedding, didn't she?"

Suddenly Skye wanted to think only of the bad things about Reanna. Maybe that was so she wouldn't have to look at the miserable part of her own self. "I have to take Babe and Floyd and Twinkie with me when I go."

"Why do you have to go, Skye? Why don't you just stay here with all of us? You know how much we love you. Stay here until Reanna and Bill finish what they're doing and come back."

Skye shook her head. She couldn't stay there where every time she looked at the old orchard she'd be reminded of what she'd done. But even if she went, the wounds would still be there inside her, like the grooves the cougar's claws made on the logs of Sweetie's cabin.

"Popcorn's ready," Jermer said. He handed around a big bowl of hot, buttered popcorn.

For a while there was only the sound of crunching. Then Skye said, "The funeral was real nice. I can't believe all those relatives came for just a little kitten."

Sweetie smiled. "They didn't come for the kitten, Skye. They came for you. That's what a family is all about."

Skye slept that night after all. She lay there on the daybed in Sweetie's kitchen, listening to the fire sputtering to itself in the stove. Listening to old Mangler purr as he slept at her feet. Listening to the creaks of the old house. Thinking about the cougar who had scratched on the wall and about all the people who'd lived in this little valley and all the things that had happened. Wondering before she slept if any of them had ever been as darnfool dumb as she was.

She didn't cry until she got back to Grandpa's house the next morning and saw Floyd and Twinkie asleep in their box. They slept in the same tangled little knot as before, but now part of the knot was missing.

All because of her.

That's when she cried. She cried so much, repeating over and over what a stupid, no sense blockhead she was, that Grandpa got worried.

"Wish I knew what I could do for you, Sis," he said, handing her the big blue bandanna he always carried in his back pocket.

She'd hurt him, too, she knew, trying to run off the way Reanna had done all those years before, leaving only a note behind. She knew he'd seen the note, but he hadn't said anything about it.

"Everybody makes mistakes," he offered when Skye went on crying. "Not a one of us who hasn't done some whoppers."

"Not as bad as me." She honked her nose into the big bandanna. "Aren't you going to say anything to me about trying to drive off with Reanna's car?"

Grandpa nodded. "Yuh. I'll get around to that. But not while you're feeling so down on yourself."

"Grandpa, help me find Reanna," Skye said. "I want things to be the way they used to be. I want to be with her. Right now. Unless she doesn't want a total mistake like me any more either. Will you take me, Grandpa?"

SEVENTEEN

GRANDPA STOOD THERE LOOKING AT HER FOR a long time before he said, "I guess I could take you to find Reanna, if you're sure that's what you want to do."

"I'm sure," Skye said.

He nodded slowly. "I was hoping you'd get to like it here, Sis. I was going to say you could keep all of them cats, if that would make you happier. We'll take them to the vet in Preston and get them fixed so there won't be any more kittens. Then you can keep them all."

"I like it here, Grandpa." She realized that was true, and for a moment she thought about staying. She'd be able to apologize to Cody for using him the way she'd done. She hoped they could be friends again. But then there was Denise, who'd probably never be her friend even though they were cousins.

On the other hand there were Aunt Esta, bossy

168

but fair, and the other aunts. There were Sweetie and Jermer. And Grandpa. And the kittens. Even Brad Rasmussen, who might be a real tiger after all.

"I have to be free, Grandpa," Skye said. "That's the way I have to live. I have to be free with Reanna."

He took in a deep breath, then let it out in something like a sigh. "All right. We'll go, soon as we know where to head."

Skye started to tell him they'd very likely find Reanna and Bill in American Falls on the Snake River. But he held up a hand. "Tell you one thing, though," he said. "I'm not a-gonna let you go off feeling the way you do about yourself. So let's have a bite of breakfast, then I'll take you to visit the only people who never make mistakes."

"Is Aunt Esta one of them?"

He smiled. "No, Sis. Wait and see."

Before they left, he gathered a bouquet of summer flowers — asters and cosmos and three spikes of blue delphiniums. He stuck them into an old blue quart mason jar, which he handed to Skye as they got into his battered farm truck.

Tarzan came along, sitting on the seat between them like a third person. He smelled of the barn, but he was warm and happy and Skye liked having him there.

They drove along the country road, between the tall stands of sunflowers. Skye figured she'd always think of Sheep Creek when she smelled the rank, weedy odor of them.

They went past Aunt Esta's house, and Aunt Belva's, too. Grandpa turned left when they came to the church and drove up the hill behind it to the cemetery.

She should have guessed he was taking her to the cemetery. Where else were there people who didn't make mistakes? But she hadn't seen Grandpa's joking side before, so it was a surprise.

She couldn't help but laugh a little, and that pleased him.

"Thought you might like to pay your respects to your Grandma Abby anyway before you up and go away again," he said. "I like to bring a few of her flowers to her every week or so."

They all got out of the truck and Tarzan immediately went off sniffing gopher trails.

Grandpa took the flowers from Skye. "Over here," he said. "Here's where she is." He stopped on the way to fill the mason jar with water from a faucet near the roadway.

Skye walked over to the gravestone that read: *Abigail Smith Rallison*. She removed a jar full of wilted flowers to make room for the fresh ones Grandpa set down. "Tell me about her, Grandpa. I don't remember much about her."

Grandpa took a little folding knife from his pocket and hunkered down to dig some healthy-looking dandelions from the grass on the grave.

"She was a lot like you, Sis. Pretty brown hair. Blue eyes. A real good person. Liked cats and people. Smart. Like you." He brushed some dirt off the gravestone. "Sometimes I can't hardly believe she's gone. I miss her so dang much."

His loneliness surrounded him, so heavy and gray that Skye had to turn around and look at something else. A few yards away Tarzan barked at a bird who mocked him from a nearby tree. Skye walked toward him, looking at grave markers.

"Are these relatives of yours?" she called to Grandpa, not so much because she wanted to know as that she wanted to get his mind away from his grief.

Snapping his knife shut, he got up and came to stand beside her. "Relatives of yours, too, Sis. Over there's the little boy your grandma and I had, died of meningitis when he was barely walking. And there's my dad, stubborn cuss he was, and my ma. Wish you could of tasted her soda biscuits. There's my dad's folks and there's my granddad's brother who died in World War I."

He spoke as if he were introducing them to Skye, those people who'd once walked through these same valleys and hills. They'd left behind the old house where Grandpa lived and their pictures and their blue eyes, which showed up in a lot of their kids and grandkids and great grandkids. Like her own blue eyes.

As Grandpa spoke, she got the feeling he was stitching her to the family, just as surely as Grandma Abby had sewed her likeness to that family history quilt on Grandpa's bed. It scared her a little, as if those stitches were binding her to this place. But mostly it made her feel the way she'd felt in the truck, with Tarzan warm by her side.

She walked on, reading names from the markers. One had the name Golightly on it. Jermer's last name.

"Grandpa," she said, "is Jermer's mother here somewhere?"

"No, Sis. There's some kin of hers here, but she's buried up along the Snake River someplace, where her and that man of hers lived when Jermer was born." He gazed out over the valley. "Jermer's ma, she died a-birthing him. His pa never did let him forget it. Told him all the time how he put his ma in her grave. Pretty messed up, Jermer was, when Sweetie offered to take him." Leaning over, he pulled up a weed. "He's okay now. Sweetie, she's the kind can love the hurt right out of a person. Jermer's not related to her, but she can make family of anybody."

Skye remembered Cody saying that you didn't have to have the same blood to be family. She was beginning to understand what he meant.

Grandpa whistled to Tarzan. "Guess we best be getting on home. Feeling better now?"

"Yes," she lied.

She didn't feel all that different. But at least now she understood a little about Jermer and why he thought of graves all the time. She understood how things that happened could leave their mark on a person just as surely as that old cougar had left those grooves in the logs of Sweetie's house.

There were three things sitting in the yard when they got home — Jermer and two black-and-silver Harley-Davidson motorcycles.

EIGHTEEN

JERMER WAVED ENTHUSIASTICALLY WHEN HE saw Skye and Grandpa. "Skye," he yelled, "guess what! Reanna's here, and Bill, too."

Reanna had come back! Skye had known she would. It had taken longer than Skye had thought, but that's the way it was with Reanna's elastic time.

Skye tumbled out of the truck even before it stopped moving. "Reanna," she screamed.

"They're in the house," Jermer said. "Going to the bathroom and stuff."

Skye ran up the porch steps and almost collided with Reanna, who was just coming through the door.

"Reanna." She wanted to grab her and dance all around the porch but wasn't sure Reanna would like that. "I knew you'd come back for me," she said.

Reanna reached out and gave Skye one of her

quick, hard hugs. "It's great to see you." She held her at arm's length. "I've missed you a whole lot. How've you been?"

"I've been terrible, Reanna. I did something awful." Before Reanna could even ask what it was, Skye told her about running over little Oh with the station wagon.

Bill came out of the house while she was telling about it. He put an arm around her shoulders.

"Poor Blue Skye," he said when she finished. "That's really tough."

Reanna nodded in agreement. "I'm sorry, baby. But don't feel so bad. It was only a kitten."

"He wasn't *only* a kitten, Reanna. He was *Oh*. Jermer named him that. He had these marks on his back like overalls, and his little face was so funny it made a person laugh. I wish you could have seen him."

"I do, too, Skye." Reanna's voice took on a stern note. "But what I want to know is what you were doing driving the station wagon alone."

"I was going to go find you," Skye said. "I can't stay here."

Grandpa had come up to the edge of the porch, and Skye was sorry he had to hear that.

"I mean," she said, "I have to be with you, Reanna. I'm so glad you came back."

"Skye, look." Reanna cleared her throat. "We didn't plan to take you with us now. We just came to see you before we go on to Nevada."

Skye stared at her. "You *have* to take me."

Reanna sighed. "Skye, we detoured over a hundred miles just to see you. I don't want to hear any sass now."

Skye's heart began to speed up. She had the feeling that if she didn't talk faster, Reanna was going to escape before she could even tell her how it could all work out.

"We can take the station wagon, Reanna. We can all ride in there, and I can take Babe and Floyd and Twinkie. Those are the cats that are left. They can ride in the back, and I can ride back there with them so they don't crawl around all over, and they won't yowl and scratch if I'm right there to keep them calmed down."

She paused for breath.

Reanna was smiling as if something were funny. "Skye, Skye, what pipe dreams. We can't travel with cats. They'd hate it, and so would we. You know that."

Skye slumped.

Bill still had his arm around her shoulders. "It's hard being a kid, never having a say in anything. I remember how it was." He looked over at Reanna. "Blue Skye has had a pretty rough time."

He stopped. He and Reanna gazed at one another, messages passing between them even though no words were said.

"Please let me go with you," Skye whispered, almost afraid to speak.

After a moment Reanna said, "I really have missed you, Skye."

Skye waited.

"We've always got along all right before, haven't we, honeybun? You haven't been too deprived, have you?"

Skye held her breath.

Reanna clapped her hands. "Okay, come with us, Skye. We'll put you in school when we can manage it. I really do like to have you with me." She paused, then said, "But no station wagon and no cats. You can ride behind me on my motorcycle. Grab your duffel and let's go."

"Yay!" Skye hollered, jumping down from the porch and doing a little dance around the motorcycles. "Yay!"

"Now?" Grandpa hadn't said anything before. "Are you going to take her off right now? I thought you might have a bite to eat, maybe stay the night."

Reanna shook her head. "We have to be on our way, Dad." She and Bill started toward their motorcycles. "Get your stuff, Skye, while we do a little rearranging on our bikes."

"I'll be just a minute." Skye danced up the steps, then stopped, looking at Grandpa. That gray loneliness was all around him again. "Grandpa?" she said. "Will you be okay?"

He nodded slowly. "Sure, Sis, I'll be fine. You go on, if that will make you happy."

She was going to ask him if he'd take care of the kittens but decided not to. He had so much to take care of already. Maybe it would be better if she didn't say anything at all, if she didn't know what was going to happen to the cats.

"I'll be right down," she said to Reanna as she ran up the stairs.

She didn't realize Jermer had followed her until he said, "I'm going with you, Skye."

"Don't be silly, Jermer." She snatched up her jacket, her map of the western states, her comb and toothbrush and stuffed everything into her duffel.

Jermer stood in the middle of the room. "I've got my backpack here with my eggs and stuff. I'm all ready. I can ride behind Bill."

Skye didn't even answer him. She didn't have time for this. She zipped her duffel shut.

Jermer blocked her way when she turned to go. "Take me with you, Skye. Please."

She stopped and took a deep breath. "Why do you want to leave here? You said you like it at Sweetie's."

"I do. But if you go, there won't be anybody to play with. And I have to look for somebody, remember? I think it's my dad, or maybe the lady who used to like me." His face bunched up as he tried to recall something. Or somebody.

How much did he remember about the father who'd said such awful things to him?

But was that her problem?

"Jermer, listen," Skye said firmly. "I'm really sorry, but look at what happened to Oh when he tried to follow me." She put her duffel strap over her shoulder and pushed gently past him.

"Skye, don't go." He clattered behind her as she started down the stairs.

Skye could hear him start to sniffle. She'd never heard Jermer sniffle before.

"Skye," he pleaded.

"Jermer, stop it."

At the bottom of the stairs she turned to face him. Before she could say anything, he threw his arms around her waist. Now he was outright bawling.

She tried to unwrap his arms, but he held on tight. She tried to disentangle herself by walking backward, but he stumbled along with her.

"Jermer," she said. She touched his hair, which he — or maybe Sweetie — had combed neatly before he'd come there this morning. "Jermer," she said again. Her hand ran down the back of his neck and over the hump of his backpack, ending up on his shoulder. "I have to go now," she said gently.

Jermer rubbed his face across her front, and she was sure he'd slimed her blouse because the bawling made his nose run.

"If you're going, why can't I?" His voice was choked and muffled against her middle.

"Because," Skye said.

She could feel him stifle a sob. "Because why?"

"Because you can't go running all over the place looking for something when you're not even sure what it is." Outside, she heard the motorcycles start up. "Because it's good to have a place that's home." She stopped to look down into his face. "Because there are tons of people here who love you, and that makes you very, very lucky, Jermer."

The two kittens chased each other around the table legs. Through the door Skye saw Grandpa standing on the porch, his shoulders sagging. Grandpa, who wanted her to stay but said it was okay for her to go if that would make her happy.

"You can't go, Jermer, because . . . because . . ." She couldn't think of any more becauses.

Except one. "You can't go because of all the soft, sweet things here that need you."

She knew she was talking to herself then, not Jermer. All those reasons, hadn't they been building up inside her ever since she came?

There was so much to leave.

So what if she stayed? What was she missing? Riding around on the back of Reanna's motorcycle? Where did that get you except to another place that a lot of the time wasn't too different from the last place you'd been?

What else? The grimy motel rooms? The

smoky campgrounds? What about the freedom? Wouldn't she miss being free?

So what exactly was being free? Maybe the freedom came in being able to make the choice for yourself.

"Skye," Reanna called. "We're leaving. Hurry."

It reminded Skye of another day a couple of weeks ago when Reanna had called out the same thing. Skye had been coming downstairs that day, too, carrying her duffel.

She hadn't had a choice then.

She put down the duffel. Taking Jermer's hand, she took him with her as she walked slowly out to the porch to stand beside Grandpa.

"Reanna," she began, then stopped to swallow before going on. "Reanna, I was thinking maybe I'd rather stay here anyway."

"Don't kid around, Skye," Reanna said. "Just get on behind me and let's go." She made a motion toward the back of her motorcycle.

Jermer's hand tightened around Skye's. He scrubbed the other hand across his nose.

"I don't want to go." It surprised Skye to hear herself saying this.

Reanna gave an exasperated sigh. "Well, why the big dramatic act then, all that yowling about wanting to go with us?" Her eyes narrowed. "Are you trying to lay a guilt trip on me?"

"Reanna." Bill reached over to put a hand on Reanna's arm.

She shook it off. "I'm tired, Skye. I'm not in the mood for whatever it is you're trying to pull. You said you wanted to come with us and I said it's all right. So let's go."

Skye straightened her shoulders. "You always said if we found a place we liked a lot, we'd stay."

Reanna nodded. "Yes, I did. I haven't found that place yet."

"*I* have," Skye said.

Reanna's face was getting red. "Skye, I'm your mother. You'll do what I say."

"I've always done what you said." Skye tried to sound calm. "I've gone with you everywhere *you* wanted to go. It was okay. I liked it. But now I want to stay here. You *said* I'd like being part of a family if I'd give it a try."

"You're defying me, Skye."

"No," Bill said. "She's just growing up."

Reanna turned on him. "You stay out of this. Skye, for the last time. Get on this motorcycle."

"No."

Reanna opened her mouth, then closed it again. She revved the motor of her bike.

Skye pulled her hand gently from Jermer's. She walked slowly over to Reanna.

"That's more like it," Reanna said. "Now get on."

"Skye." Jermer's voice was full of pleading.

Skye put her arms around Reanna. There was a fragrance about Reanna, clean and woodsy with a little smokiness mixed in, like the faint scent of a campfire.

"Good-bye," she said. "I love you, Reanna. But I'm going to stay home."

She wondered what Reanna was going to do. Reanna liked to be the one who said what was going to happen.

Reanna sat stiffly for a long moment. Then she sighed. "Okay. So I've been dumped." She kissed Skye softly on the cheek, something Skye couldn't remember her ever doing before. "I'll be back, Skye. Soon."

Soon. That elastic word again.

Reanna started her Harley moving.

"Good-bye," Skye said again. "Good-bye, Bill." She was quite sure that it would be a long, long time before she'd see them again.

Then they were gone, roaring off down the road toward the blue hills that separated Sheep Creek from the rest of the world.

Skye and Grandpa and Jermer stood there on the porch until the noise died away.

Fumbling in her duffel, Skye pulled out her tattered map of the western states.

"Jermer," she said, "I don't need this anymore. How would you like to have a funeral for it?"

Jermer's face glowed. "I'd like to do that. I've got something I don't need, too."

He reached into his backpack and brought out three brightly colored eggs, one purple, one green, one yellow.

Skye took them from him, surprised at how light they were. "How long have you had these in your pack?"

"Since Easter," Jermer said. "Not the last Easter. The year ago Easter. That's when I came to live with Sweetie."

Skye caught Grandpa's eye, and they both smiled.

"Jermer," Skye said, "let's all go see if Sweetie wants to come to the funeral. Then the four of us can come back here and I'll fix Hamburger Helper Hurrah for dinner."

She knew Grandpa had hamburger in the refrigerator, and she'd seen a box of Helper in the kitchen cabinet where Aunt Esta kept putting the cereal boxes. You made it Hurrah by adding almost a whole bottle of ketchup and a dash of tangy mustard.

"How does that sound, Grandpa?" she asked.

"It sure does sound mighty fine." He shuffled his feet. "I'm right happy you're staying, Skye."

It was the first time he'd ever called her Skye. She remembered that he'd said it wasn't good to give a name to something you couldn't keep.

She was glad she'd decided to fix Hamburger Helper Hurrah. This was a day that called for something truly special like that.